NO WAY OUT

Soapy was beginning to hope he might have lost his pursuers when a tiny geyser of water erupted right in front of him. The sound of the shot had been too far away to notice.

Creeping up the rim of the cut, he searched the landscape. Tiny puffs of smoke located the shots for him, and there were more of them now, whizzing into the turf close by. They were coming from several rifles and carbines up on the last ridgeline before the descent into the valley.

He slid back down until his boots were in the mud, pulling his pistol from the holster and then realizing the futility of that. Hunkering in the streambed had seemed like a good idea, the only idea at the time, but it had resulted in his being trapped. He huddled against the bank, trying to think his way out, listening to the shots going overhead.

If they couldn't hit him, or the horse—and so far that didn't seem to have occurred to them—they would eventually come down, encircle him, and the only place you would find Soapy Smith thereafter would be in a dime novel.

DEVIL'S
CREEDE

JAMES DAVID BUCHANAN

LEISURE BOOKS   NEW YORK CITY

A LEISURE BOOK®

September 2005

Published by special arrangement with Golden West Literary Agency.

Dorchester Publishing Co., Inc.
200 Madison Avenue
New York, NY 10016

Originally published as *Welcome, Suckers*.

ISBN 0-8439-5569-4

Visit us on the web at www.dorchesterpub.com.

DEVIL'S CREEDE

Plenty of silver
Plenty of greed
Welcome, Suckers,
To the city of Creede.

—Cy Warman,
editor, *The Creede Candle*

Oh, Jesse had a wife,
She mourned him all her life...

—From a ballad attributed
to Billy Garshade

Prologue

I have it in my mind to recite here a tale about an adventure in the life of a famous man of the West, and I will do it. I suppose "infamous" to some of you poor creatures who follow the common herd, which causes small-mindedness. Pinheads, I call them. But I will say no more in that regard since even his worst enemies would not have failed to recognize the subject of my story as a true gentleman, whatever else.

I have plenty of reasons for setting down this story of a time that is gone forever but was one hell of a time in its time. One, I am getting old, damned old, and you have a lot of odd thoughts then. Fact is I can hardly see the paper, so I am telling it to somebody who can. They will fancy it up some, I expect, but not too much.

I am not mad about being old. I should have died forty years ago, and here I have lived to give witness to them driving autos, flying æroplanes, short skirts—God bless them—and the biggest god-damned war you ever heard of. I have truly seen wonders.

Anyhow, the important reason: I have read books and pamphlets about this gentleman, name of Randolph Jefferson "Soapy" Smith, and none of them has got it right. Names, places, events, they are all pitifully muddled and contradict each other something fierce. I wonder if anybody knows? But what they have done is a downright disgrace to that noble calling of *belles-lettres*.

Now, he was no angel, Soapy. If he was, you would not

want to hear about him—am I right? So it is my promise to you that I will not honey-coat him, not one bit. Also, I do not claim every single word you are going to read here is the honest-to-God's truth, either—where's the fun in that?—but it is *my* truth and the only one you are going to get. If I wasn't somewhere, don't you think I'll make it up? Anyhow, everybody out of short pants knows writers are the biggest liars since hector was a pup.

Never mind who I am. None of your beeswax.

Chapter One

Soapy had never attempted to flim-flam an entire country before and it was proving a mite more difficult than even his overly rich imagination had conceived.

"They will be the roughest, fightin'est, ridin'est badmen in the West. But I can manage such men . . . I've done it . . . an' I promise yuh, suh, tuh weld them inta a troop so redoubtable they will stand up tuh a regular army ten times their number. Lick 'em good, too. Hannibal 'g'inst the Romans. Washington 'g'inst the British. Lee 'g'inst the whole damn' Northern Army. Go ennawhere, fight enna one. . . ."

Smith had a mellifluous voice to go with his refined Deep-South drawl and showed a graceful but driving enthusiasm in everything he put his hand to.

The old general, dictator of Mexico, *Don* José de la Cruz Porfirio Díaz in full blazing uniform bearing enough medals to blind a regiment, strode through the palace halls with amazing vigor and a perennial scowl.

"Colonel" Smith, a naturally handsome man with a black beard, on his part not wanting to lay on the dog overly much, was wearing a severe, dark suit, silk cravat with diamond stickpin (his last bit of capital in the world), and military boots. Normally he would have had a pistol on his hip, but one dared not in the presence of His Excellency.

Although taller, Jeff Smith was finding it difficult to keep up and pitch at the same time. He was more accustomed to marks that stood still with their mouths agape and greed lighting beacons in their eyes.

"Yes, yes," the general cut him off, using English, "you explained all this earlier, Colonel. A Mexican foreign legion. An excellent idea."

"Like the French, we would make no inquiries inta the recruit's background. Their past is their own. All we ask of 'em is loyalty untuh death tuh the legion. And Yuhr Excellency, uh course."

Impatiently the *caudillo* waved a hand, signaling enough! Glancing at his gold watch, he picked up the pace.

"Yuh understand, *Señor Presidente,* I meant no negative reflection on yuhr own magnificent *rurales,* but only as an adjunct. . . ."

The old man gave him an impatient look, a half snarl, and began walking even faster.

Jeff had reason to curse himself inwardly. He couldn't seem to stop pitching, even though he knew better. Distracted, he nearly failed to return the salute of a palace guard, standing rigidly against the wall in a golden breastplate and helmet from the Napoléonic era. The *presidente* ignored him.

Finally they arrived in a gallery with huge, arched windows where Díaz was satisfied to stop and look out. Jeff followed his gaze down to a lovely garden with a fountain, neatly defined walks bordered by varicolored tropical flowers, jonquil, hibiscus, bougainvillea. He thought maybe the general was checking on his gardeners or simply admiring what they had produced, and for a moment his hopes rose.

Nothing like a lovely garden to bring calm, although you didn't see a whole lot of them in his profession. Then, at the far end, something of a shock, his eyes found a wooden post driven into the ground in front of a brick wall. Two uniformed soldiers in blue and red Frenchified uniforms with kepis were dragging a man in that direction. His white shirt

12

and pants were torn, dirty; his bare feet left a trail of blood on the stones of the pathway. Behind them came a silent drummer.

Without actually looking, Jeff noted that *Presidente* Díaz again consulted his watch and emitted a sigh of pleasure, apparently at the punctuality of the events below. How fortunate they had arrived on time.

Jeff had seen a lot of men die, had killed a couple himself, yet he didn't very much care for violence, didn't trust it. And executions cut a little too close to the bone.

"The money you asked for yesterday."

So that was it. "Yes, suh, Yuhr Excellency. Eighty thousand. . . ."

". . . American dollars," the general finished it for him. "A not inconsiderable sum for a poor country like ours, a madhouse ravaged by famine and revolution, wouldn't you say so?"

"Yuh must remember, General, while these men are of an elite breed, I will still have tuh train an' equip them like. . . ."

"You must think I am a fool, Colonel. A man I have never seen before with a plan that may never come into being. You are impressive, yes, but I will have to look more closely at what you propose before anything is paid. I promise you, if you please us in this, you will have no complaint about your treatment."

Below, separated from them by glass, distance, and the indecent splendor of just about everything, the condemned man was tied to the post, sagging as if someone had cut his strings. The squad of soldiers marched up to confront him and an officer came forward to offer a blindfold. It was refused with a shake of the head, and the drummer began his death roll.

Jeff was disinclined to look at Díaz, afraid that he might be

13

smiling. "I'll have tuh have somethin' tuh start up with, Yuhr Excellency. These men are used tuh bein' paid handsomely an' they'll surely expect a signin' bonus. Perhaps I could get by for now with somethin' a good deal less, like ten thousand, but it will not. . . ."

"Two. You will accept two and that will prove sufficient for the moment."

Events in the garden moved swiftly now. Commands were given, the squad lined up, and fired, the shots barely discernable above the drum roll. Jeff had his hand on the glass and thought he felt a vibration but maybe that was his own heart.

The victim's body seemed to leap upward within its bonds, then fell back and twitched alarmingly. The officer commanding quickly came to deliver the *coup de grâce*, appearing to find it as distasteful as did Jeff.

"Later," the *presidente* said, "when they have cleaned up down there, we will take a little walk in the garden . . . it's beautiful, don't you think? You will have the money then and I will tell you what I expect for it."

Jeff was still watching the scene below. "Revolutionary?" he asked. "Rapist, murderer?"

"Accountant."

The general left him there.

Later, Jeff had his little walk in the garden with *el presidente,* who had little to say in the way of warning. He had, after all, made that point earlier. His aide handed over the two thousand dollars, so apparently the telegraph had yet to bring back the evil news of "Colonel" Smith's total lack of any military experience beyond organizing a band of hoodlums to defend the Denver city hall against the depredations of a reformist governor.

14

The rest of the conversation was surprisingly friendly on the *caudillo*'s part, a fact that Jeff found sufficiently alarming to send him hurrying in search of his diplomatic aide, Gentleman Syd Dixon, immediately afterwards. Syd was the one-time scion of a wealthy Eastern family who had fallen from grace and gone on the pipe, not necessarily in that order. Smith, tolerant of just about every vice that didn't include roasting babies on spits, still found uses for him when he was clear-headed. In fact, Syd had done quite a good job portraying a former U.S. senator in the first couple of meetings, before he had succumbed overnight to the glowing fleshpots of the city. That was another problem with Syd: when he wasn't on the pipe, he was on the girls.

Fortunately, when Jeff finally found him, it was not in a hop joint, only a low *cantina* in a poor section of the city, a venue so far down the social scale that no respectable Díaz spy would even consider entering it. Syd did have a flinty-faced *señorita* under each arm and a bottle of *pulque* in front of him, but, thank God, his eyes were normal.

Jeff ordered a full pot of violent, perfectly awful Mexican coffee. The *señoritas* were paid-off and sent on their way. Syd waved and groaned as he watched them go, but this was the boss.

"We-all are leavin' Mexico," Jeff said, moving closely to him in the booth and speaking softly, making it look casual. The smoke, a lot of it marijuana, was so thick it hurt his eyes and throat, and both were used to a lot of smoke.

Syd coughed in sympathy. "Soon?"

"Now."

Syd, always elegantly dressed, extracted a gold watch fob from his vest pocket and consulted it as if for wisdom. "That's real soon," he said. "Kind of a long walk, though, isn't it?"

"He's lookin' inta us with the telegraph."

"That damned telegraph again."

"It's an invention from hell. I'll agree with that. Drove ol' Cassidy an' Sundance right out uh the country uh their birth, an', don't yuh know, that's downright unAmerican."

"How'd you know he'd found us out?"

"When he started actin' nice. We had us a friendly little stroll in his garden not an hour ago. He actually put his arm 'round mah shoulders."

"Oh, oh."

"Worse, he had tuh reach up tuh do it. I went a little bow-legged, but I could still feel the damn' epaulets diggin' in halfway down tuh mah elbow."

Years on the grift made for a keen psychologist—Gentleman Syd understood perfectly.

"Talked sweet, made a lot uh promises an' even called me *amigo*. Hell, ever'body in Mexico knows when *el presidente* gives yuh the embrace of eternal friendship, they're already diggin' yuhr grave somewhere."

"We get any money at all out of the ol' bastard?"

"Not a whole lot, an' he didn't think he'd even have tuh part with that. When I was out uh the room, they'd changed the lock on the wall safe where they thought I'd put it. I asked one uh the toy soldiers there for the new combination an' he said I'd have tuh ask *el presidente* who kept 'em all in his head. Remarkable man to do that."

"So we got nothing?"

"Two thousand American."

"How'd you get it out?"

"I never put it in. I used some newspaper tuh make a Chicago roll an' put that in the safe. Money's here"—he patted his waist that was a little thick on a lean man—"minus the twenty I needed for the roll."

16

"Not much, considering we're flat."

"I know." Jeff shook his head. "But he had me watch an execution earlier. I do believe the gentleman regards it as a form uh recreation. Some poor devil stole money. An' don't yuh just think he might've been tryin' tuh tell us somethin'?"

Syd slumped in his seat, surrendering to reality.

"This here's a land uh dire consequences, Syd, an' we knew that. So, if we get out with our tail feathers intact, it'll at least give us braggin' rights and a fair step up somewheres else." Soapy, the proven optimist, had taken charge.

"Where? Can't go back to Denver."

"Tuh get back tuh Denver we'd have tuh still be alive, so let's talk about just gettin' *somewhere*. I got it all planned. You go first, 'cause they been seein' a lot more uh me. There's a train leavin' here in an hour an' a half for Vera Cruz. Yuh can catch a steamer for Brownsville. They'll never figure yuh for goin' east. Ennaway, I'll be leadin' 'em north."

"Jeff, I can't let you do that."

"Sure, yuh can, 'cause yuh don't tell me what tuh do." The tone and smile were easy but not without resolution.

"How do you expect to get out?"

"I been over tuh the Department uh Transport and Transmission an' got me a map uh all the telegraph and railroad lines. All I got tuh do is ride between 'em."

"Ride what?"

"Oh, I figure 'bout midnight I'll wander down tuh the stables . . . *el presidente* goes tuh bed at nine, yuh know."

Syd was shocked. "*Nine* o'clock?!"

"He's got that superb white stallion called César in there. Was showin' it off tuh me, an' I've had mah eye on it. Ever since I was a trail hand in Texas, I've favored white horses. He's a real beauty."

"You're gonna steal that horse? He loves that horse like a

woman. He's the president of the god-forsaken country. He'll stake you out on an ant hill."

Jeff smiled, a truly charming smile when he wanted to use it, part rascal, part enveloping and part affection, although he really had none, save for his mother. His loyalty and generosity were legend, but affection?—not so anyone would know.

"If he catches me, won't make much difference, will it? I forged a note on some paper I slipped off the old man's desk, sayin' I was authorized tuh take César out on a secret mission. Sweet thing is, there's an iron rule . . . nobody dares tuh wake him up when he's sleepin'. Be worth a man's life."

Syd couldn't stop shaking his head. "Aw, Jeff, don't go against a stacked deck."

"Listen, now." He put his hand on Syd's arm and felt trembling under the skin, nerves and muscles screaming for the pipe. "I'll be well on mah way tuh the other coast by that time, then turn north."

Syd could only murmur: "You'll never make it. Good Lord, boss. . . ."

"I'd have yuh put on a little disguise, yuh're good at that, an' don't try tuh take ennathin' with yuh. Yuh understand? Don't go near the palace. Here. . . ."

Jeff looked around the room and, satisfied, reached under his shirt, fumbled around a little, and finally slipped Syd a wad of cash under the table. "I counted it . . . 'bout a thousand. Yuh got yuhr pistol?"

"My Derringer and a buck knife."

"Have tuh do. Yuh go easy now. Stay off the hop an' ever'thin'll be fine."

Jeff started to get up and Syd reached out to grab his arm. "Where am I supposed to go, Jeff? What are we gonna do?"

Syd sounded so plaintive Smith almost laughed. "That's

18

right. I didn't tell yuh, did I? Creede. I'm even sendin' for the boys."

"Where is it?"

"Colorado. Don't yuh ever read the newspaper?"

"I never heard of it, but I don't like the sound of it. What's there?"

"What's not there's the telegraph."

"That's a start."

"Rich veins a silver. Huge mountains of it. Pure as yuhr mother's eyes."

"I heard that about a lot of places."

"Dammit, son, where's yuhr faith?"

"Soapy, I'm older than you are."

"Hell, what's this caper here mean? Don't mean biscuits in the grand scheme uh things. What's always been there, Syd, when we-all have had tuh ride inta a sunset only to come out at dawn full of piss an' vinegar? Riches and glory, man! Riches an' glory for the takin'. The whole world's ours to plunder. Now, buck up."

Syd had been inoculated against Jeff's grandiloquence and grumbled: "More'n likely hell's there."

Smith slapped his shoulder and stood up. "Yuh can't cheat an honest man, isn't that what we always said?"

"Yep."

"Yuh believe it?"

"Yep."

"Well, it's generally known the devil's not an honest man. That's how he got tuh be the devil. We can handle him. See yuh in Creede."

Chapter Two

Gentleman Syd Dixon proved to be a prophet in suggesting that Creede and hell would have a lot in common. Not all of the inhabitants might have agreed, especially those who were having too much fun getting rich and spending it, but the general population was surely headed in the right direction for a good long parboil. Squeezed increasingly tight and narrow by high cliffs on two sides, one over-reaching Eastern journalist had described Creede as a cleft in the devil's chin.

It was two months before Jeff Smith arrived at this remote corner of the southern Rockies near the headwaters of the Río Grande. It would have been hard to say which was the worse for wear, the horse or Jeff, the saddle and bridle, or his dark suit turned shiny from so much wiping and brushing. The man and horse, both ordinarily proud creatures, sagged and dragged their way up the steep trail. The horse was doing a better job of living off the land than Jeff, who could do that only if it bore people ready to point to the walnut with the pea under it.

The first sign to announce Creede contained an arrow that pointed straight up. He groaned and the horse broke wind in a similar comment. They paused only a moment, pulled themselves together, and continued their struggle along the steep trail through clusters of spruce and fir.

The next sign announced: **Stakes In Snow Don't Go.** The scenery was beautiful in this mountain springtime with everything that grows showing signs of colorful bloom yet with small patches of shiny white snow reclining on the slopes on either side. Jeff wasn't much on scenery, though, and he had a lot on his mind.

A mile or so farther on, he was surprised to catch sight across a meadow of some telegraph poles, many still bearing mangled wire on their double crossbars, uprooted and thrown into careless piles. Smith went off the trail and circled amid the débris, curious. Some poles had been burned. There were also two graves nearby but nothing written over them to tell the story of who had died. Some serious violence had been done here, that much was obvious.

Another sign a little farther into the pass, where it was noticeably closing in so that he was beginning to feel a touch of the indigenous claustrophobia, actually cheered him up. It read:

PLENTY OF SILVER
PLENTY OF GREED
WELCOME, SUCKERS
TO THE CITY OF CREEDE
Signed: Cy Warman, Ed., *Creede Candle*

That spoke to Soapy Smith and sent him on his way, grinning, for the next half mile, until he heard the sound up ahead of rushing, tumbling water. That kind of stream at this altitude could be dangerous, especially in the horse's present condition, and he had to hope there was a bridge and not a ford.

His first view of the riotous stream confirmed his suspicions, but then, fortunately, he saw the bridge. Unfortunately there were two armed men, standing on it, who must have heard him through the trees as he had come up the trail.

"Hold up there, mister!" the tall one of the two called to him as he approached.

"Gentlemen."

"We ain't no gentlemen, and this here's a toll bridge. Don't come no farther 'less you can pay."

They wore derby hats and worn city suits and ties, blunt faces and blunter manners. Both had Remington repeater rifles, the short one with it on his shoulder as if on guard duty in the Army, which is where he had probably learned it. The tall one, piratical with glaring piggish eyes and a large scar running down his cheek into his beard, slung it under his arm. They were types with which Jeff was all too familiar, dimwitted and for that reason all the more dangerous.

He tried to work up some of the old Soapy charm through the grime and fatigue, all the while edging the horse down to the foot of the bridge, and dismounting.

"How much is that now?"

"Five dollars."

Jeff shook his head. "That's a mighty big toll, boys. All I got in the world's five dollars. How 'bout a little high-card draw? Double or nothin'?"

The guards laughed to each other. "That's all Creede needs . . . another sharper," the tall one said.

The short one didn't want to be left out: "This here bridge's the only way 'cross that's safe. Try swimmin' it, you'll freeze your keister. More'n likely you'd get kilt."

Leaving the horse loose on the bank, figuring it was too tired to wander, Jeff eased out onto the bridge. It was wooden, built high and wide on piles, but without guardrails.

The tall one waggled the muzzle of his rifle at the holster on Jeff's right hip. "Don't get no ideas 'bout that pistol, slick. Drop your belt."

Smith unhitched it and let it fall at his feet.

The short one had his weapon off his shoulder now to make it two being pointed at Jeff's vital organs.

Jeff quickly put his open hands up, part way. "Be easy now, boys. Be easy. I kin see as how I'm out-manned here. An' ennaways, I'm a peaceful man. Yuh just might uh heard uh me . . . the professor with a high degree in the teachin' uh the evils uh games uh chance. I'm known far and wide, as mah whole plan in life's tuh demonstrate tuh people how gamblin's destructive tuh the human spirit an' bank account just by rubbin' their noses right in it. Prove to 'em how they can't win so's tuh send 'em back tuh their wives an' little children tuh sit by the hearthstone, better an' wiser for the experience. I kin see already I've come tuh the right place."

The tall one looked aside at his partner, face crunched in confusion, and asked: "What kind of horseshit is that?"

The short one said: "I don't know, but you better pay or git, Mister Professor." He put his repeater to his shoulder and aimed, even though Jeff was only about ten feet away.

The tall one said: "I think we oughta take his horse, too. Bring a good price."

"Good idea. Long as we give Bob his share, he won't mind."

"All right, boys, 'nuff funnin'. Can I reach in mah pocket for the piece? Without y'all shootin' me?"

The tall one said: "Just be slow, *reeeal* slow."

"Tell yuh the honest-tuh-God truth, men, I only got this one coin. I hate tuh give it up. Worth a lot more'n five dollars. It's a genuine Spanish doubloon given me by mah old pard, Porfirio Díaz, *el presidente* uh Mexico. It pains me terrible tuh lose somethin' as valuable as this antique money just tuh cross a damn' little bitty bridge."

He held up the much-polished coin to catch the sunlight.

"Look at that. Look how it does shine. Take this tuh anyone, they'll tell yuh how it's solid gold an' five hundred years old." He grinned at them. "Bet yuhr boss never sees this, huh? Which one uh yuh gits it now? Wouldn't want tuh start a fight 'tween yuh two. Here!"

He tossed it high in the air so that it would land between, or behind, them. The guards spun and scrambled, reaching up desperately, snarling like starving dogs at a lamb chop, slamming into each other. The short one dropped his rifle in order to use two hands, and still it ended up on the wooden planks at their feet. By the time they recovered their sense of duty, Jeff was standing there with his pistol leveled at their midsections. He might have been pleased with himself but he wasn't smiling.

"I come a helluva long way tuh be shivereed by carnival trash like yuh boys. Put the gun down easy an' pointed away from me. Don't yuh think for a minute I wouldn't put a bullet in yuhr foul guts an' laugh doin' it."

They looked frightened and with good reason. Jeff's black eyes showed an ugly heat that might consume them any instant. The short one had a pistol in his belt and was told to drop it.

"Stand with yuhr backs tuh me, facin' the water. Close it up, side-by-side. Put yuhr toes over the edge, that way I won't have enna trouble."

"You gonna kill us?" the short one whined. " 'Cause, mister, I got a wife and little kids back in Saint Louis."

"Yuh all do when it comes tuh dyin'," Jeff said as he picked up and threw their weapons into the water on the opposite side. "Who thinks he owns this damn' bridge, ennaway?"

"Mister Bob Ford," the short one said in a trembling voice.

"Never heard of him."

"You will." The tall one could still scowl. "He runs every damn' thing around here."

"He did," Jeff said, putting his gun back in the holster.

"He ain't gonna be happy 'bout this."

"You, neither." He gave the tall one a vicious kick behind one knee and gave the short one a push between the shoulder blades. Both went together, screaming and flailing, into the turbulent water only to disappear beneath it. Jeff stood for a moment, watching them be swept away.

Waving, pleading hands above the froth and cries for help from downstream decided him that this was not his idea of entertainment. Maybe they would turn up on shore somewhere, proving that they could swim, although not many did out here.

When he turned away to go back for his horse, he spied the coin lying on the planks. "Keep the change," he murmured to the waters, tossing in the coin in hope of absolution.

Chapter Three

When you got close to a mining town you could smell the miners, hear them, feel them. The first sign, naturally, were the claims on the surrounding slopes. It was along toward evening that came early here because the mountains cut off the descending sun before its time. Yet you could see the miners working hard, and many of them would still be at it by lantern light when it was wholly dark.

Jeff caught the eye of one whose claim was down closer to the trail and waved a friendly greeting. The man's response was to grab up his rifle and stare at him. Jeff kicked César forward and moved away a little faster than he had come and with a better idea of what to expect.

He had been in a lot of these places and they all looked pretty much alike, except for what nature provided. In this case the town was built in a narrow defile with a creek running through it. There was an Upper Creede and a Lower Creede with all kinds of self-proclaimed boroughs, but the names had changed so often it didn't pay to learn them. To most people it was simply Creede.

Wooden buildings were everywhere with boardwalks and muddy-rutted streets heavily decorated with horse manure. There was no church, school, or bank, but a livery stable, sheriff's office, a couple of two-story hotels, assay office, teamster yard, general store, café, a kind of hardware store that sold mining equipment mostly. It was a noisy place, teamsters shouting at their beasts or for people to get out of the way, construction going on even at this hour. There were more saloons than all the rest of the buildings put together, some advertising entertainment, even floor shows. As usual, there wasn't nearly enough housing, so tents, big and small, were located wherever there had been open ground. Some of these, too, were saloons or little makeshift brothels usually with one or two slatternly girls.

Jeff rode in at twilight, grateful to be anywhere. His second impression was that here was an amazing amount of light, noise, music, screaming, quarrels, hilarity, a lot of drunks getting an early start on the evening. Wagons and riders, too, seemed disproportionate in numbers to the size of the town. There were a lot of gaudy women, almost none of the settler variety, and some young boys but no children. Not surprising, only a lunatic would have brought a small child to a place like this, although they would come.

He was looking for a particular establishment on the main street but stopped his horse to listen to a group of people that did include a couple of plain, stout women with shawls, gathered around a fire, singing what was apparently a local song:

> While the world is filled with sorrow,
> And hearts must break and bleed,
> It's day all day in the daytime
> And there is no night in Creede!

After this they all broke into raucous laughter. Jeff supposed it was a kind of civic pride in the licentious nature of the town. He could work with that. Oh, yes, he could.

In the next block he went by a pitchman of unusual appearance—long hair and beard, tall and thin, almost emaciated, but very brown, a tan applied every morning from a bottle. Around his feet were prominently identified jugs and

27

bottles of honey, or at least so labeled, but they were of a suspicious color. He was dressed only in shoes, pants with galluses, and a top hat. Appropriately he was known as Yankee Hank Fewclothes, and from atop a wooden crate he was expounding in a singsong voice:

> *The red man knows the natural way.*
> *It's roots and berries keep pox away,*
> *But the purist of all for nature's money*
> *Is the sweet elixir of God's own honey!*

"Look at me boys"—he pounded his chest—"like the red man I need no shirt or coat. Why? I live with the natural heat of the forest that comes with beautiful golden honey. What little I do wear is not for warmth"—he tipped his hat —"but out of respect for the ladies."

Jeff, still on horseback, laughed, and the pitchman gave him a quizzical look but never paused in his recital.

"Like the little animals of the plains and mountains, cruelly exposed to the blast of winter. . . ."

Smith went on until he spotted the particular business he had been seeking, a large tent with a sign in front that advertised:

F. Green
Barber to Kings and Queens

Jeff grinned when he saw it. Dismounting, he pulled the poor, lag-footed horse toward the hitching post in front.

Before he had taken two steps, there was a roar from within the saloon across the street, rather predictably named Bonanza, and a man burst through the swinging doors, propelled by something violent, screaming something unintelli-

28

gible. Young, in work clothes, he leaped off the porch, but that was as far as he got. At the instant he hit the dirt street, a bulky bartender with a shaved head and a full mustache wearing an apron slammed through behind him with a shotgun.

Jeff instantly let go of the horse and threw himself into the muck from instincts honed in dozens of cow towns and gambling halls. He got there just as the bartender fired.

The fugitive, hit in the back, was driven forward, his body arched like a bow, but a bow in flight. He spread out his arms when he dove to earth.

The bartender blew the smoke out of the shotgun, spat off the porch, and went back inside with criminal insouciance. Only now did people begin to reappear on the streets.

Jeff was up quickly and went to the victim, who was moaning and writhing in the mud. There were a dozen wounds or more in his back and, fortunately for him, none in his head. No wound appeared to be deep, but collectively they drenched his shirt and the top of his denim pants in blood.

Smith looked down at him for a moment. No one else was ready yet to come close. Jeff was trying to decide if he should get involved in something he knew nothing about, thus violating one of his basic rules. But one of his other basic rules was that there was no way for any reputable thief to make a living in a town without some kind of law and order. This last decided him. He knelt and ripped the man's shirt off, what was left of it, and shouted to the onlookers, now creeping closer, to get a doctor. He scanned the wounds from top to bottom. When he started scraping and probing, it elicited bellows of complaint. Afterward, Jeff looked at the blood on his hands with distaste.

"Hold on, pardner. Only birdshot. Yuh might even live

29

if y'all quit squirmin' an' yellin'. Town's noisy 'nuff as it is."

He went over to César and got a bottle of whiskey—Rocky Mountain antiseptic—from his saddlebags and brought it back to pour over the man's wounds, bringing more howls of pain.

"Yuh go an' get yuhrself shot, son, least yuh could do is shut up 'bout it."

A fat man in a swallowtail coat, carrying a black bag and with strong liquor on his breath, waddled up to them and introduced himself as a doctor. It was not a hopeful sight. "May I have a sip of that, sir? Carry me through the next hour it'll take to pick these little beauties out, one at a time. Damn, if I didn't have queens and jacks, too."

After a swig, the doctor began his examination with trembling fingers. "Blood poisoning does pose a definite concern here. Well, I can make more money in less time if he dies, and just maybe be back in the game where I was twenty-five dollars ahead. See, I'm the coroner, too." He seemed to find this amusing and chuckled.

When the wounded man heard, his groan was so loud people thought there was an elephant in town.

Jeff stood and looked down. "Yuh sure yuh're a medical doctor?"

"Absolutely, my friend. Although I do handle horses and mules as a profitable sideline."

In a very soft but deliberate voice, Jeff said: "Look at me, chief. I promised this young man he would live."

The doctor looked up into eyes unexpectedly but convincingly cold and hard as black diamonds. He murmured, not daring to look any longer: "He'll live."

"If he don't, yuh ol' whiskey soak, I'll come lookin'."

The doctor got the idea. Timidly he asked: "Who's going

to pay my bill. I've seen this boy around town and he don't have diddly."

"I will. See me over there."

He pointed at the barber tent, which caused the doctor to wince and murmur: "Yes, sir."

Jeff could have that effect on people, even if for the moment he was a king without a country. He tied off the horse and removed the saddle, leaving it on the ground. But instead of going to the barber tent, he headed for the saloon where the shooting incident had originated. He went through those same swinging doors, seemingly without a care in the world.

In other circumstances he would have been delighted by what he saw—riotous play, gambling, dancing, music, loud talk and song, and drunks spending money in the best here-today, gone-tomorrow spirit of every boom town with their pokes sitting on the bar. You would never know there had been a shooting within the last few minutes, but that was no surprise.

Jeff spotted his man immediately, a voice as loud as a cannon. He had already switched to a bung starter and was flourishing it in front of an old, white-haired man at the bar who looked poorer than the kid and was sweating and trembling while he counted out his money, small coin by small coin.

Jeff went over to where he could hear the conversation

"I don't want all that little horseshit," the bartender snarled, looking at it with ferocious contempt. "In here, men pay with greenbacks or silver, you old bag of gas."

"I don't know if I have enough for him, too?"

"You come in with him, you pay for him."

"I just met him out in the street."

"Barkeep," Jeff said quietly, and was ignored.

"And you seen what happened to him," the bartender said

to the old man, who by now had emptied his pockets and was ruefully regarding the contents, the few small coins, a crumpled letter, a rabbit's foot, and a key with a ring bearing a medallion engraved with the words **Home Sweet Home** surrounded by flowers.

"Barkeep."

He turned to Jeff with a scowl. "Hold your damn' horses, there, slick."

"I got a real important message for yuh here."

The bartender's look of doubt and suspicion, really a scowl, gave him the aspect of a rutting moose. "What are you talkin' about? Who from?"

"Belle."

The old man was now paralyzed but fascinated, looking from one to the other. He appeared to understand what the bartender couldn't, the underlying drama of mongoose versus cobra in Jeff's soft voice and bland manner.

"I don't know any ding-dong Belle."

Odd, Jeff thought, since every saloon in the West seemed to possess at least one. "I'd try an' think real hard, friend. Maybe she gave yuh another name. 'Cause her three brothers just got out uh Yuma an' they're sure as hell lookin' for the fella that done her wrong."

By now the man's face was screwed so tightly it seemed doubtful that he could talk or even breathe. "Three brothers? I ain't done nothin'."

"Maybe that right there's the problem."

A couple of miners and a whore down the bar were watching them, hoping for some excitement, anything. Several other customers were yelling orders to the bald bartender whose name apparently was Gus, but he was hooked now and had to know.

"All right, what's the message?"

"Not somethin' yuh'd want all these people tuh hear, I wouldn't think. Lean close."

Jeff himself barely moved to meet him so that the man had to cantilever his own body across the bar, putting himself distinctly off balance. He growled: "Yeah?"

Jeff regretted his adversary's lack of hair. It would have made things so much easier. He took second best and grabbed hold of the right end of that formidable handlebar mustache with his left hand and yanked. Unfortunately the man had a heavy center of gravity and most of the hair came out in Smith's hand. Meanwhile, his right hand was whipping the Colt out of its holster and bringing it up to the battle. While there was no longer enough hair to hold onto, Gus had let out a shout of pain and careened halfway over the bar simply to reduce the pull.

Jeff had enough momentum to get the muzzle of the gun jammed into the soft flesh under the man's chin to the point of almost breaking it open. That blow stopped him dead for a moment, and now Jeff threw his left hand, still full of hair, around behind the head to pull it farther forward.

He bent Gus's ear and hissed into it: "I'll shoot right through yuhr damn' brain, yuh understand, chief?" Gus moved his head up and down to the extent the pressing muzzle allowed. "Start movin' an' no talkin' tuh enna one."

The only response was something that sounded like gargling, his breath sounding like a steam engine warming up.

Jeff turned his head slightly to the old man, whose mouth was hanging open. "Time tuh go. Git! Take yuhr money."

The old man grabbed up everything in front of him and ran out on bowed, ancient legs, cackling to himself.

By now the room had gone quiet. There were still a few drunks and hard-core gamblers who wouldn't have noticed Judgment Day. Jeff started the two of them moving sideways along the bar toward the entrance. Still bent over, Gus reached one hand up to feel where he had formerly worn one half of his self-esteem. Feeling the bristle and open spaces brought a tiny whimper.

"Hey, you, what the hell's this?" one of the dealers, in sleeve guards and with an eye shade, yelled at him.

That set off a chorus: "You got no right . . . that's Gus there."

"Yeah, you leave the bartender alone."

"Who's he? I never seen him before."

"Looks like a dude to me. Tenderfoot."

"Hell, he's a sportin' type. Anybody can tell that."

" 'Nother of them sharpers, that's sure."

Jeff raised his voice, one accustomed to public speaking, careful to keep it friendly. "I'm arrestin' this man for attempted murder, like enna public-minded citizen of a decent town has a right tuh do. . . ."

"How long you been in town?" a big, prosperous-looking man demanded.

"Ten minutes," Jeff snapped back with a grin, "but I settle in fast." He got his laugh.

By now he had Gus around in front of the bar and lowered the gun to his waist. The bartender was bleeding under the nose, blood dripping across his lips, and he kept swiping at it unhappily with one hand. He was sufficiently down from his former ferocious self for Jeff to let go of him and have a Derringer slip out of his sleeve into his other hand. He kept it out of sight because it wasn't going to impress anyone and might even have the opposite effect.

"I personally witnessed this bully shoot a young man uh the town in the back while that lad was fleein' for his life."

"What business is it of yours, big mouth?" a miner in the crowd called.

"Suh, I'm not a man uh violence, but I do like tuh wager now an' then, an' I'm willin' tuh bet a hundred dollars at two tuh one odds that yuh will not come out uh that bunch, walk right up tuh me like a gentleman, and say that tuh mah face. Enna one want tuh take that bet? I should tell yuh I'll kill 'im."

There were some nervous laughs at that, but still some shouted offers and waved bills, the kind that would bet on a cockroach race. Jeff spun his Colt one way, then the other, then back and forth so fast that it was simply a blur. To him it had nothing to do with shooting, but was merely another form of the legerdemain upon which he had built his whole career.

"It's all in the hands," Clubfoot Hall, the old shell gamer who had started him on his career, had told him, "all in the hands."

Feeling it still might not be enough, Jeff fired one shot and knocked the top off of a bottle at the far end of the bar. After that, the anonymous miner decided to remain just that.

Jeff resumed: "Hell, I know mah fellow Westerners. Know how they feel 'bout shootin' a man in the back, 'specially a young boy like this, who no doubt's got uh grievin', gray-haired ol' mother somewhere, prayin' her son won't ever run inta a bully like this 'un here. Never come home ag'in tuh the family hearthside, tuh the bosom of his family . . . if you'll forgive the word ladies." He got another, smaller laugh.

"He couldn't pay his bar bill, mister. Then he gives Gus a lot a sass!" the dealer called out.

"So, this man here used tuh have a mustache . . . look how big he is . . . he gives the boy a kick or, hell, a paddlin' like we-all got in school. Takes him by the scruff uh the neck an' kicks him out the door. Give 'em a lesson that sends him back tuh that dear ol' mother a better man. But yuh don't shoot him in the back with a shotgun, dammit."

A woman's voice said: "That's right!"

"I know who you are!" a man shouted. "You're Soapy Smith from Denver, by God."

"So I am, ladies an' gentlemen, an' I mean tuh stay. I like the looks uh this town an', from what I can see, all it needs tuh be a real fine place tuh live in is a little law and order. That's startin' right here."

He prodded the bartender in front of him to the swinging doors. There was a certain amount of grumbling and a lot of confused, excited conversation.

"I'm takin' yuh tuh the sheriff. Get along."

A dark-visaged man came out of the crowd that was clearly of two minds now with a bung starter in his hand. Jeff didn't bother with: "Halt." He knew better than that. He compromised in using the Derringer, pointing and firing both barrels at the attacker's legs. Moving, they made a difficult target for the pea-shooter, but one lucky round caught the man in the kneecap, shattered it, and toppled him forward with a yelp of pain.

"Like I said, folks . . . law an' order." Jeff touched the brim of his Western hat and left the stunned crowd behind. The last thing he heard was someone hurling a name after him: "Bob Ford!"

Chapter Four

Sheriff Ord Herkimer was a gangly, easy-going sort, about sixty. He could have used a shave, a haircut, and a bath, and had the look of a man who might even get one of each in the next year if he woke up in time. His feet were crossed on the desk, wooden chair tilted back, eyes closed under his Stetson when Jeff pushed Gus inside. They remained closed for a few seconds while he stirred himself.

"That the sheriff?" Jeff asked his prisoner.

Gus growled something that sounded affirmative.

The office was a shabby little cubicle with a single cell behind it, holding a sleeping drunk. When Herkimer rose, brushed himself off, and grinned, Jeff asked him if he was the sheriff.

"That's me. What've we got here? Gus again?"

"Yuh're not wearin' a gun," Jeff persisted.

"That's so. If I did, somebody might shoot me."

Smith was going to let that go as hopeless, but changed his mind and decided to deliver one of his stump speeches on the efficacy of law and order, winding up with the suggestion that it was seldom achieved without resort to firearms. The sheriff nodded and stared at the desk, as if taking it all in, while vigorously digging into one ear. He asked exactly what it was that Gus had done. Jeff described it.

"Yep. I heerd that shootin' out there a while ago. Sounded like a shotgun. That you again?" he asked Gus who only glowered. The sheriff shook his head.

"If yuh heard it, why didn't y'all go out there?"

"Mister, there's so many of 'em in this town a man'd wear himself out if he chased after ever' one. Say, Gus, what happened to your mustache?" He turned to Jeff: "He had the finest handlebar you ever did see, best in Creede . . . won a contest with it."

"This bastard tore it off," Gus accused, "and I want him charged."

"With mustache tearing?" the sheriff asked, scratching himself. "I don't think that's in the book, Gus."

"Just lock him up, would yuh?" Jeff said, getting a little tired of it all. "I'll see tuh the trial." Anxious to get on with his own bedraggled affairs, he started out the door.

"Trial?!" The sheriff seemed to find that amusing. "Mister Ford, he don't like trials. They make him nervous."

Jeff stopped. "Who?"

Gus came to life for the first time since Jeff's assault, laughing in the same nasty way he did everything. "He don't know. Let him find out."

Jeff, shaking his head, walked back to the barbershop. Darkness had fallen and the town was livening even more, brighter and noisier, more people on the muddy streets. As he trod through the same mud, this little hole in the mountains took on a wonderful presumption, pound for pound brighter and more active, wilder and more raucous than the Barbary Coast. His kind of town, waiting to be taken—his prayers had been answered. There was only one question. Some damned fool named Ford seemed to be in the way. It did sound familiar.

When he pulled back the flap and entered the barber's tent, there was a trio of men sitting around. One was strumming a banjo without really playing anything. Another, a straw hat over his eyes, was seemingly playing cards with himself on top of a crate. The third, the honey salesman, was pretending to read the *Police Gazette*.

They all turned and glanced at Jeff when he entered, but that was all the attention he got, although Gentleman Syd did grin a little from under the straw hat. The barber was a three-hundred-pound man called by the sporting fraternity Fatty "Shoot-Your-Eyes-Out" Green. The fat man never smiled. He had, judging by the feet, agitated hands, and city clothes, a small tenderfoot under torture in his improvised barber chair, buried under towels and rags, none of them too clean, while he wielded scissors and comb as if they were saw and claw.

In a voice like a St. Bernard, although less benignly, Fatty growled: "You say you want the works? Friend, that's what you git 'round here."

The man's little feet and hands flailed in the air. "I . . . didn't . . . *blub, blurp* . . . say . . . *mumpf* . . . I wanted. . . ."

Another huge pile of towels landed on his face and were held there while he nearly suffocated and Fatty hummed "Sweet Rosy O'Grady". The customer's struggles were those of an ant being trampled by an elephant. Finally Fatty relented long enough to let in a little air accompanied by some words to the wise.

"Partner, up here a man keeps his word once given. You said you wanted the works, now, didn't you? You tellin' me that ain't right?"

The man moaned between gasps for breath.

"Good. Don't go changin' your mind ag'in. And stop your damn' wigglin'. I'm an artist. I take real pride in what I do." He pushed the towels back down on his victim's face, but stuck his big ham fist in to grab the man's nose and pull on it to make certain he could breathe. Stepping over to the tent wall, he flipped the price card over and a haircut went from twenty-five cents to two and a half dollars and everything else proportionally.

While working the pump at the sink, Fatty turned to the other men sitting around the tent. "I tell you, it's jist awful hard for a laborin' man to make an honest livin' these days."

Jeff said: "I can see that. 'Specially the way yuh do it."

That got a laugh from everyone but Fatty and his victim.

Syd signaled with his eyes and a toss of the head for everyone to follow him. They went out through the back flap into an adjoining shack where there were cots and some primitive living facilities.

Yank Hank, still in his shirtless state embraced Jeff like a kid would a long-lost parent, calling him "Soapy". Gentleman Syd grinned, shook his hand, and expressed his relief that he had gotten out of Mexico alive. Banjo Parker, an immense, sleepy-eyed man with his instrument forever on his back, slapped Jeff on his so hard that it was all he could do to stay on his feet.

The first thing the others wanted to know was what had happened out there on the street? Jeff gave them a hasty account, anxious to get on to the business of the moment.

Yank Hank was worried. "That bartender, that Gus, he's a bad one. Real flinty, mean. You should've settled him, Jeff. He'll be your enemy for life."

"If I settled ever' enemy I had, the country would be severely depopulated." While speaking, he looked around. "Where's the old man, where's the Rev or Doc Baggs or the Judge . . . ?"

"The Rev was last seen in Elko," Yank said. "We sent him a telegram 'fore we come up here, but we didn't know you wanted the whole gang."

"Go down an' send for him again. I can see already where

hard times got us by the throat an' we're gonna need help tuh get loose."

Gentleman Syd said: "I heard you went through Denver. Any luck?"

Jeff shook his head, pulled a poster from an inside coat pocket, and unfolded it. "They're fresh out uh luck in Denver . . . an' so are we."

As Fatty came in from his barbering, got a bottle from under his bed, and began pouring glasses of whiskey to hand around, Jeff showed it to each in turn.

WANTED FOR BUNCO AND MAYHEM. There was a pretty good illustration of an elegant "Soapy" Smith and a long list of his gang members, including the four in the room.

"Never mind, boys, the good times we brought tuh Denver are their loss now. An' we've started from scratch before." He took his glass from Fatty and raised it in a toast. "Creede's the place. We're gonna own this town, I promise yuh that. Won't be a one uh us don't leave here a millionaire. . . ."

Outside, there was suddenly a lot of shouting and shooting. Jeff paused while it went on, everyone looking to the front.

"Jist somebody killin' somebody," Fatty said.

Jeff looked appraisingly at his compatriots. "What's the matter? I heard this was the biggest strike since Leadville? Bigger."

"Oh, it's that all right," Yank said. "The Holy Moses Mine alone's giving a hundred tons a day."

They all knew that, still it brought whistles, sighs, and exclamations.

"Problem is," Banjo said, and it was rare when he said anything, "Bob Ford got here first. He's got some mean 'uns workin' for him."

Gentleman Syd said: "He owns the town, Jeff, lock and stock."

Yank Hank said: "Got a regular monopoly, all right, on everything we do best."

Fatty downed his whiskey in a gulp and was pouring himself another. "Cain't skin hog sweat off these miners after Ford's done with 'em."

Jeff shook his head. "All I hear lately is that same damn' name. Wait a minute. Yuh don't mean the little weasel that shot Jesse James in the back ten years ago an' went on the vaudeville to whistle 'bout it? Not him?"

"Him," Syd said.

Yank had an even gloomier view. "Only he's not real little. He's not in vaudeville. He's in the runnin'-things business and he's an awful good shot. Turned up a lot a toes since Jesse, he has."

"Does when he comes out," Syd amended, "but mostly he stays holed up in that saloon of his. He's scared to death some friend of Jesse's down in Missouri's going to show up one of these days."

"Jesse was real popular," Jeff said a little wistfully, "that's certain."

"Carries three guns most of the time when he does go out," Banjo said. "And that rough bunch around him goes with him."

Jeff, disgusted, sank down wearily on a camp stool. "Don't they have any decent law 'round here? Someone we can bribe?"

Syd shook his head. "They got a town council, but they're afraid to give Bob any guff."

Jeff shook his head. "Well, we're sure as hell runnin' out uh towns."

He grew pensive and the others waited him out. He was

42

always the man with the plan.

"We need money," Jeff announced. "I got my tripe and keister on the horse. Enna one got a stake?"

Everyone consulted their pockets or wallets and turned up a few tens or twenties. Syd had a few hundred.

Yank was shocked. "Soapy, you're surely not going back on the street? Why you were practically King of Denver."

"I'm not proud. 'Sides, it's good tuh keep yuh hand in now an' then."

Even Fatty was worried: "Bob Ford don't allow no competition no how, Soapy. You gotta git a license and give him a cut."

"They're right, Soapy!" Yank could warm to any subject. "We all had to buy his damn' permit and pay a tithe to keep it. But with your reputation, he's not likely to look on you with favor. Like Banjo says, he's got himself the ugliest bunch of dog-kickin', mother-beatin', baby-shootin' yahoos you ever did see."

Jeff thought about that, too, for a moment, while the boys awaited his inspiration. Then looked up with that special grin which could charm saints or sinners, priests or killers, nuns or little girls, but was merely one more weapon in the arsenal.

"Sure . . . but I got yuh fellas." He stood. "Fatty . . ."—he said, heading for the barber tent—"the works."

Chapter Five

The next night Jeff set up his game at the quieter end of the main street where it led out of town, not by choice but out of prudence. The bright lights and loud noises of a typical Creede night were at least a block away. Fortunately he had a loud voice that didn't sound as though he was shouting at you.

All gussied up, he stood tall, thumped the display case like a drum, and demanded attention, bellowing: "Come on, boys! An' ladies, too, if there are enna. An' even if there aren't, any female's welcome an' got a God-given right tuh be just as fresh an' lovely as those snobby, nose-in-the air, blue-blooded ladies back East. More, 'cause she's here and we love her, don't we, boys? Here we go now! We're gonna clean up Creede!"

Gradually people began to drift down the street to see what was going on. Jeff continued the pitch, mixing sarcasm and humor, until he had a large enough audience to be profitable. Now the approach was quieter, more personal.

"Boys . . . I hate tuh tell yuh this. Mah mother . . . God bless that wonderful woman . . . didn't raise me tuh utter un ugly word 'bout one uh the Lord's creatures, no matter how low . . . but I got tuh say, y'all are the worst-lookin', evil-smellin' pack uh back-hill mud-wallowers I ever did see. Mah horse didn't lead me inta Creede. Mah nose did."

The crowd grew. Some laughed at his impertinence, but a couple seemed ready to fight, so Soapy worked his famous grin to lighten the tone and hold them off a bit. "Now that's a downright shame, 'cause underneath all that dirt an' dust, mud an' horse manure, I'll bet there's some noble souls listenin' tuh mah message right here, right now. One or two ennahow. There's one. There's 'nother, I declare."

He indicated a newcomer and pretended to be speaking to everyone but him. "*Whooaa!* Is that there a man just come up or a buffalo? *Whooeee!* A wet buffalo at that."

He had them all laughing at the bewildered newcomer. Time to flip open the display case revealing . . . a mound of soap, each bar wrapped in opaque tissue.

"But I've got just what it'll take tuh set yuh right, boys. It's not silver or gold makes the swell . . . it's soap!" He held up a bar with one hand, and with the other displayed a hundred dollar bill. He lowered the bill to show it to a couple of his closest listeners. "That's right . . . soap! An' yuh see what I'm doin' right here. I'm puttin' this hundred dollar bill, U.S. currency, right in that wrapper there, an' puttin' the soap back in the pile."

He wrapped a couple of other bars in different denominations. "I'm shufflin' 'em a little bit so's I got at least a fightin' chance uh not goin' home in mah union suit. This soap yuh see here, pure as mothers' milk an' manufactured in the beautiful city uh Paris, France, cost twenty dollars a bar over there an' I'm makin' it available tuh the public for a pitiful five dollars. It will transform yuhr lives. Women will fight over yuh. Governors an' princes will invite yuh tuh dinner. Even better, there's that hundred dollars in there somewheres, an' fifties an' fives an' ones an' twenties. I give yuh mah word."

The crowd was showing the usual signs of an incipient greed growing beyond reason.

Soapy had his back to them, but just entering the town at the other end of the main street were a band of horsemen, big, ugly, unwashed, squinty-eyed men on horses of the same kind. They were distinctly not miners but rather cowboys, wearing sheepskin jackets and heavily armed—Goths, Visigoths, Vandals . . . predators.

"Now who'll start it off? Who's the sport? Pay five, win a hundred. Don't be shy, step right up. . . ."

He was interrupted by a cry from the crowd: "I'm your man!" Yank Hank, acting as capper, pushed his way forward, brandishing a five-dollar bill. "I'll try you, mister. You took all my business, anyway."

"Here's a man who'll take a chance. If yuh boys are not willin' tuh take a chance, what the hell yuh doin' in Creede, ennaway?" Then aside to the crowd: "Bath wouldn't hurt him enna, neither . . . am I right?"

"Don't believe in baths. Dirt protects, like honey."

Yank carefully scanned all the soap in the case, almost but not quite touching the individual bars one after the other. The crowd became very quiet. Suddenly Yank grabbed a bar, held it up to eye level, unwrapped the paper, and produced a fifty-dollar bill. With a yelp of pleasure he raised it above his head.

"How do you do! Fifty dollars!" He did a little dance, waving it around. "See there, sharp eyes come from eating honey." He ran off, still flourishing the fifty.

"There's a winner. Mah loss." Soapy looked appropriately stricken. He should have. The Huns were approaching slowly, but they were getting closer.

"Who's next . . . who's next?"

The crowd pressed in eagerly now, pushing each other out of the way, many brandishing fives and pleading for a chance, some throwing their money at Soapy. A man bought a bar, found a five inside, and was thrilled, telling everyone in sight, most of whom agreed that it was marvelous. Others got ones with less enthusiasm, but some of those bought more cakes in the hope of hitting it big this time. Still, the mad buying went on faster than Soapy could take in the cash and stuff it away.

In minutes most of the soap was gone and the crowd had dwindled. Always a few people hung around, just watching as if it was a sporting event, which it was. But Soapy, in his eagerness to right the ship, was slow to spot the change of mood that had come over them.

"Hold on, boys, whatever's the matter here . . . ?"

A horse neighed behind him and he stiffened, keeping his pose for the moment. The crowd began to back away nervously.

"Well, say, now, if it ain't Soapy Smith."

Jeff turned slowly, and, as he did so, the horsemen moved out around him. He greeted the speaker with a hard, charmless smile from another part of the arsenal.

"Hello, Kelly."

Kelly had the kind of crooked-toothed, rancid smile that flings its insincerity in your face, all defiance and ugly thoughts. He was lean and sun-baked, rather a lined face for so young a man, with long, stringy hair. Tiny eyes gleamed like a puma's in the moonlight.

"You know me?" he drawled. "Now that's sum'pin'."

"Rincón Kelly. Worked for Hi Wilson up at Devil's Creek."

Kelly turned to the boys. "This feller run pret' near all of Denver. I was in that Tivoli of his oncet. You was lucky to git out with your britches. I figure he still owes me for that." He turned to Soapy with mock pity. "Must be awful hard times bring you back down to street hawkin', Soapy. Kind of sad. . . ."

Jeff had considerable ability to stay calm in the face of threat. Still, he brushed the handle of his Colt to see if it was loose in the holster. "I don't mind. Meet a lot uh interestin' people."

Kelly laughed. "An' so you have tonight, so you have. Us . . . ain't we interestin', you cheap slick?"

Soapy was about to let them know that they were pushing him a bit too far when one of the other riders, an ape named Lev, but an ape who still looked a lot smarter than Kelly, edged his horse over and signaled that there was someone coming.

It was Sheriff Herkimer on a bicycle, unarmed as usual. He pulled to a stop in the midst of the horsemen, took off his hat, and scratched his head. "Somethin' wrong, boys?"

Lev said: "He's new, Sheriff, and he don't have no license."

Soapy tipped his hat to the sheriff. "Mah apologies, Sheriff. I didn't know there was such a thing. How much is it?"

"Twenty dollars."

Soapy dug into the cash and silver jammed in his pockets and extracted a twenty, handing it to the sheriff.

"Can I go on with mah business now?"

Kelly's face scrunched up, creating a hundred new lines of prairie desiccation and turning his eyes into tiny, malevolent insects. "*Whooa*, now, he cain't git away with nothin' like that. This here's a bunco."

"It's a game uh chance, just like any other in this town."

"Horseshit." Kelly, Lev, and two others dismounted and moved over to the display case. "Go through that," Kelly told his men, "and show him." He explained how Soapy had promised that some of the bars were wrapped in large bills. "One was s'posed to be a hunnert-dollar greenback."

As they unwrapped each remaining bar, they threw both soap and paper into the mud at their feet. Soapy looked on

48

calmly. None of them contained any money until one of the band yelled derisively: "One ol' horseshit dollar." He held it up for the sheriff to see, then crammed it inside his shirt.

Kelly turned to the sheriff. "See, there's no hunnert in here." He slapped the case, knocking it off the tripod. "There never was nothin' 'cept a couple of them little ones. It's a bunco. So, you can arrest him legal, like Bob likes, or we're gonna drag him out of town by the feet and maybe he'll fall into a cañon." He turned to the remains of the crowd who had been Soapy's customers. "Say, maybe we should start cookin' us up some tar, whattaya say, fellas?"

The crowd showed some enthusiasm for that idea. It would be a show.

Soapy's response was to ease his hand back to the pistol grip. "On a cold day in hell . . . ," he started to warn, when someone came pushing into the group, calling out: "Just a minute here, just a darn minute here, gentleman!"

When everyone looked to see who was claiming their attention so vigorously, Soapy worked the hundred dollar bill out of his sleeve and palmed it.

The new arrival, Gentleman Syd Dixon, drew not a hint of relief from Soapy. "Sheriff, I won that hundred." He turned to Soapy, extended his hand—"I want to thank you, mister."—and received the hundred, palm to palm.

"First damn' luck I've had since I came to this town." He turned back to the sheriff. "Tell you the honest-to-God truth, I didn't speak up sooner 'cause, well, I owe some money. You know how it is."

The cowboys were beginning to curse and grumble. They didn't know exactly how they were being conned, but they sensed that somehow they were losing.

"I know how it is!" Fatty shouted, bulling his way in to Syd, looking hard and mean, which was no chore. He grabbed Syd's wrist and appeared to wrest the hundred from him violently, Syd wincing as if in pain.

Fatty addressed the sheriff with his usual glower: "He owes me this here hunnert, and then some. And I'm takin' it." Still glaring, he stomped off with the bill clutched in his meaty hand.

Lev had more or less figured it out, but a little late in the day. "Kelly, we been flim-flammed. They're handin' that thing 'round."

Kelly looked at the dissolving crowd in something very close to an appeal. "You hear that? They made fools of us, all of us." However, the sizzle was gone and apathy dominated the tired, dull faces remaining.

Kelly turned on the sheriff. "God dammit, Herkimer, you let him loose, we're gonna kill 'im."

"No, you're not, Kelly, not out here after all the fuss. You know how Mister Ford feels 'bout drawin' attention to hisself." He started shooing the crowd, including Soapy, away. "Go on, go get drunk, get your ashes hauled, throw your money away if you got any. Shops closed here. Scat."

Soapy announced to the remaining customers: "No hard feelin's, boys. Soap's free for enna one wants it."

A couple of men tried to scramble and pick up as many bars as they could, but Kelly remounted and led his band in a ride over it, crunching the soap and bumping Soapy out of the way. For a moment Soapy lost the control he had fought so hard to maintain and reached for his pistol, but the sheriff put his hand on his forearm, catching his eye.

"Law and order, I believe you said."

Soapy relaxed a little, watching the riders slouch away.

"I can see how that there would be somewhat bitter on the tongue, but would you fellers please jist get out of town. Boothill here's awful crowded."

As soon as the sheriff was gone, Soapy rescued the tripe and keister and started back in the direction of the center of town.

Fatty, Syd, and Yank Hank were waiting nearby in case the situation got desperate. Yank had a two-by-four in hand, Syd a grip on the Derringer in his jacket pocket, and Fatty was holding a .38 Smith & Wesson that he normally kept hidden in the very large small of his back. Banjo was absent, having fallen asleep, something he did a lot of, maintaining it was perfectly logical that the more flesh you possessed, the more it needed to rest.

Those awake were relieved to see the boss coming back in one piece.

Yank grinned and offered his hand. "Sure got interesting, down there."

Soapy wasn't to be distracted. Handing Yank the battered case and tripod, he said with uncharacteristic grimness— "We got tuh get some breathin' room here, fellas."—and promptly started off again down the middle of the street toward the center of town.

Syd noted Soapy's loosening the Colt in its holster, practically a nervous tic by now. "Jeff, where you going?" he called.

"See Bob Ford."

The gang watched him go with concern, but that was all they did—nobody dictated to Jeff Smith.

Chapter Six

His march through the heart of Creede was quiet and without gesture, but people on the boardwalks seemed to sense something, timid souls demonstrating the greatest insight. No, a man walking with that fixed stride and purpose was downright unsettling.

As Jeff neared the Exchange, Ford's saloon, the largest and grandest in town, someone hissed his name from out of the shadows between two buildings. At first, he went for his pistol, looked, and couldn't see, but something about that sibilant sound said it was a woman and justified the risk of going to find out.

A gloved hand and puff of smoke showed from out of the darkness, the smoker sitting in a buggy. He recognized the perfume before he took two steps. He should; he had given it to her.

He approached and, when he could see better, greeted her matter-of-factly with—"Hello, Mattie."—although he didn't feel matter-of-fact. There was even the tiniest quaver or throb in his voice, but Jeff would have been hard put to know exactly what it all meant.

The eponymous Mattie Silks was wearing a lot of it in her signature red that created quite a vision in the flickering, defused lamplight from the street—a beautiful face in a dark blonde setting, around thirty but looking even younger, bejeweled, long gloves delicately gripping that cigar. One black boot was up on the front of the buggy while she leaned forward.

Whatever the hidden emotion, Jeff maintained his guard in a way that could only suggest old wounds. "Been a while."

"I heard you were down south stealing Mexico."

"More like they stole me. Startin' from scratch again."

A tiny alarm bell sounded in her voice: "Not in Creede, I hope?"

"Looks like it suits yuh all right. That dress an' buggy come high."

"It's different. I'm a woman."

"Yuh bet yuh are, Mattie, an' I'll settle enna bohunk says different."

Mattie insisted on remaining serious. "Jeff, I got a solid man here."

That took a little of the air out. "Ah!" was all he said.

"Claude Parmenter. Calls himself the King of Terrors."

"Aw, hell, I know him. Fought Con Grady in Saint Louis when I was there. Grady had tuh have a new face chiseled."

"Claude fights for Bob Ford these days."

"Yuh sure hear that name a lot."

Looking past him, Mattie spotted someone. Jeff hadn't noticed, but it was the man himself, Claude Parmenter, with a head like a watermelon, fists like cantaloupes, and a John L. mustache not unlike the one that had once graced Gus's snarling face. Wearing a loud, checkered suit and smoking a huge cigar, he stood with legs spread like the Colossus of Rhodes on the porch of the Exchange and scowled in their direction.

"Could easily discourage a new man comin' in, but lucky for us, Mattie"—she saw Parmenter step off the porch with his jaw jutting and a darting eye for what was going on while Jeff started to get into the carriage—"that's just not mah style."

Mattie put out her booted foot and planted it against his

chest, sending him reeling. He cried out in surprise and indignation, finally ending up on the ground. At the same time, Mattie flicked the horse and moved it ahead to meet Claude.

Jeff, getting up and brushing himself vigorously, called: "What the hell, woman?"

Mattie was too smart even to acknowledge his presence and looked straight ahead at Claude with a frozen smile. But he knew and called over to Jeff: "You come near her again and I'll make pork sausage out of you." With a hard look for Mattie, he climbed into the buggy and drove off.

"Nice tuh see yuh again, Claude," Jeff said, to no one in particular.

More puzzled by Mattie's skittishness than angry, he happened to glance up at the second story of Ford's Exchange and there was someone looking down, grinning unpleasantly, a gaunt face with a wispy mustache. Jeff had seen sketches of that face in newspapers.

Off to a fine start, any hope of dignity already in the outhouse. Just the same, he marched into the Exchange as if he owned it. Jeff had always known the importance of creating a presence even if he had to play catch-up.

Kelly, Lev, and some of the boys were at the bar and turned to look, a little surprised themselves. Jeff nodded at them and went right past, careful not to hurry. The place was filled, loud, a lot of gambling going on, roulette, faro, poker, a girl singing at a piano, a dog sitting on the bar. A shotgun guard was on a very high stool overlooking all of this.

Having come this far, Jeff wondered how to proceed. There was only one stairway to the second story and it had a guard sitting on it. Looking around, he also spotted a large man in a red corduroy suit, wearing a derby, strolling amid the gamblers and occasionally tapping one of them or the table with his cane, delivering a message.

Jeff caught his eye and elicited a big grin as the man came forward. "Jeff Smith, this beats all. How are you, friend? God damn." Even with all that effusion he was careful to keep their meeting physically restrained.

"How are yuh, Bat?" Jeff understood well enough and shook hands formally.

Masterson signaled a bartender to get his attention and ordered two beers. He was one of the few people who knew Jeff wasn't much of a drinker.

"I s'pose y'all are one of the millions workin' for Bob Ford?"

"I'm floor manager here." Softly he added: "I saw Syd and Yank Fewclothes drift in, but I didn't say anything."

"Yuh're a gentleman, Bat. Always have been. Yuh referee the pugilism here for the man?"

"I promote 'em, too. You got an idea?"

"Maybe. Been drawin' a lot uh deuces an' treys of late."

Bat looked past him at the thugs at the bar, all of them keeping an eye on Smith, talking about him in their shiftless, dangerous way. "You shouldn't have come in here, Jeff."

"Enna chance uh yuh introducin' me tuh the boss?" He quickly put up his hand. "I'm here tuh talk nothin' but peace an' enlightenment."

Bat laughed and shook his head at his friend's audacity. "I'll try. Come on."

He led Jeff up the stairs, passing him through the guard who flattened himself against the wall to make way for them. The gang at the bar was watching, wondering what the hell was going on. Seeing Jeff look down at them, Kelly brought out his pistol and, pointing it vertically, moved the barrel up and down in that universal gesture of contempt.

Bat rapped on the door to Ford's office with his cane. "It's Masterson. Soapy Smith's here."

"He got a gun?" It was a voice like a rusty hinge.

Bat signaled for Jeff to hand over the Colt, whispering: "Sometimes he doesn't go out for a week at a time." He called through the door: "Not now!"

There was the sound of at least three locks being thrown back, but the door remained closed. Footsteps went away.

Again came Ford's peculiar thin voice: "Open it slow and easy now."

Smith gave his friend an incredulous look. Bat grinned back and eased the door open. Jeff entered warily.

The room was in darkness, but he could just make out the man back at his desk now, sitting beside a window that allowed a minuscule amount of light, making him discernable but still a mighty poor target. It did glint on the barrel of the rifle he had propped on the desk, pointed at Jeff's midsection.

"Bob?"

"Say your piece from right there."

"Bob, this isn't quite what I'd call sociable."

"I know who you are, Soapy Smith, and I'm of no mind to be sociable."

"I just came over here tuh shake yuhr hand. After all, we're in the same business, yuh and me. . . ."

"Hell we are. Not in this town we ain't."

"I don't suppose yuh'd turn on some light, bring out a bottle, sit down an' talk . . . ? No, I don't suppose yuh would. See, Bob, I'm no hell-raiser. I'm a law and order man. Yuh know that. There's plenty here for all uh us tuh steal without hurtin' ennabody. No need tuh fear me."

"Why in perdition should I fear you, Smith, when I got a Thirty-Thirty aimed right at your *cojones*. I might just pull the trigger, too. Nobody here's gonna charge me with nothin'."

Jeff had had enough. "That'd sure be different, Bob, shootin' somebody from in front."

Even in the gloom he could perceive Ford, shaking as he rose, slowly struggling to control even his voice, to stand with the rifle in his hands. "Only reason I don't is you got a name for yourself, Smith, and I don't want the word about me goin' out. But I got plenty boys'd be glad to do it and serve up your liver for my dinner." He shouted: "Masterson, get him out of here!"

Obviously Bat had been listening because he was in the room instantly. He took Jeff by the arm and tried to steer him away.

Smith resisted until he had his say: "Yuh want tuh turn yuhr back on sweet reason, that's yuhr loss, but yuh better damn' well quit this shiveree yuh been givin' mah friends."

Bob jumped up and came forward with the rifle still pointed. His face was a battlefield congested by fear and rage. He expelled words rather than saying them, so that drops of saliva reached a considerable distance to land on Jeff's clothes. "Get out of Creede, Smith!" He slammed the door in their faces.

Jeff calmed himself quickly and told Bat: "I always said Jesse was a nice fella."

Masterson maintained a strong grip on Jeff's arm, but he handed back his gun and whispered: "Go along with me. I gotta throw you out now."

"No hard feelin's."

Jeff went along with it easily and Bat let go of him, understanding it was important that his friend not look so abject as to invite ridicule. As they went along the balcony and down the stairs, Jeff asked him *sotto voce*: "How'd y'all like to be sheriff uh this town, Bat, or mayor, or enna other damn' thing?"

"Ask me when you're top dog, Jeff."

"Now that's reasonable."

As soon as they were outside, Bat shouted: "Mister Ford said don't you ever come back here!" With that, he slammed his cane theatrically against the swinging doors. Inside, music and talk resumed.

Jeff gave him a little wave and went off, feeling for the pistol in its holster. He looked around to make sure no one had followed him. The streets had quieted somewhat, and there were few miners who weren't gaming, dead drunk, or over or under a whore.

A figure appeared suddenly from behind a corner of the feed store, startling him for a moment. It quickly revealed itself as one of the ladies of the town, a pretty one. She came up and took his arm, not his pistol arm or he would have knocked her down and drawn.

"Hello, handsome Jeff."

"I know you?"

"No, but everybody knows you."

"Honey, yuh're startin' tuh worry me."

He would have disengaged from her, but she clung to him fiercely and whispered: "Somebody wants to see you. At the Library."

"Where?"

She didn't answer, instead pulled him away. He went—farther downtown, close to the end of things, not far from where he had been selling his soap. If he was compliant, it was because he didn't have a whole lot of alternatives at the moment, and she was a looker.

The puckishly named Library was a large, two-story Victorian house drenching the street in cascades of bawdy laughter, tinny music, and the effects of strong drink. If there had ever been a book in there, it would have burned up from the sheer energy long ago.

Being at the beginning of the town proper, there were no

buildings across from it where the street turned into the trail that led in and out of Creede, but there were a number of trees, one used typically for hangings, and a lot of foliage generally.

"This way." The night bird dragged Jeff around to the back.

"Y'all turn out tuh be a real good friend uh Bob Ford, honey, an' I got one in here for yuh." He touched the handle of his Colt.

"Mister Smith, gentlemen don't shoot ladies."

"I sure hope I don't mistake yuh for the other kind."

They went up an outside stairway to the second floor where the girl knocked three times. Jeff had his hand on the pistol. The door swung open to reveal a tentative Mattie Silks wearing a satin negligee, framed by a "Mauve Decade" drawing room that showed off her hair and coloring.

"Now do you feel safe?" the girl asked him.

"Hell, no."

Nevertheless, he stepped inside and the girl closed the door behind him. Once they were alone, Mattie flung herself at Jeff, throwing her arms around him wildly and clinging as if hanging off a cliff.

"Oh, Jeff, darling, why do you always go away? I've missed you so much."

Smith struggled to get loose, rubbing his chest. "That why I got yuhr footprint on here?"

"You know why I had to do it. Is that all you have to say to me now that we're alone?" She freed herself. "Bob was watching from upstairs and Claude would have had to beat you something fierce."

"Could he do that with a bullet in his heart? Yuh ought tuh know me better by now than to think I'm afraid uh enna muscle-headed pugilist. As far as Bob Ford, what's so wonderful 'bout ten years ago shootin' a picture hanger in the back an' goin' on the stage tuh brag about it? What's he done since?"

Mattie, never short on wiles, was pouting by now and had her back to Jeff. "Easy for you to say, but I'm a woman."

"That's another thing yuh keep remindin' me about that yuh don't have tuh remind me about."

He went over and put his arms around her and kissed her on the neck. She swiveled to face him and he was about to kiss her on the mouth when he noticed a large bruise. "What's this here?" Gently he brushed away the make-up intended to hide it.

She tried to turn her head away but Jeff kept his grip on her. "It's nothing. I've had plenty in my time." Her voice was a receding wave when she added: "Claude didn't like my talking to you."

He let go of her and turned toward the door. "There's very few things, Mattie, I'm not tolerant of, but this here's one of 'em. I'm gonna settle that son-of-a-bitch."

She quickly moved to block the doorway. "Jeff, wait."

He came to look at her with that intensity he could summon in a fraction of an instant, belying the every-day easy, charming Jeff to a certitude, and with some suspicion, too. "Why'd y'all get me up here, sweetheart?"

"Well . . . I mainly wanted to warn you off . . . but, also, to say I got a lot at stake here and I can't afford. . . ."

He reached out and kissed her, the kind of unapologetic, hard, engulfing kiss that is shared only by long-time lovers. At first she simply allowed him, but gradually thrust her own passion into it, and ended by struggling to pull away. "Don't. I can't. . . ."

Jeff by then was working to expand her décolletage. She started to weaken again when there was a considerable crash somewhere below. Mattie became instantly alert and trembling.

"Claude. That could only be him . . . he's mad."

Some roaring followed, then a drunk stomping and stumbling up the stairs.

"Out the window, quick." She tried to push him.

"I don't go out enna windows, honey. I'm Jeff Smith, remember?"

"Jeff, please don't. For me, then. You kill Parmenter, and Bob'll have you lynched."

"What about yuh? I'm not gonna leave yuh tuh him."

She yanked up her skirt, way up, and showed him the small, pearl-handled pistol on her thigh. She pulled it out and jammed it into her sleeve. Parmenter was already pounding on the door.

"Mattie! Mattie Silks, who you got in there, you Jezebel? Low-down, notch-flauntin' bitch! You Whore of Babylon! You. . . ."

"Now," she urged, pushing Jeff to the window.

He gave up and helped her open it. "Aw, hell." Pausing to give her a quick kiss, he disappeared outside . . . only to find himself on very skimpy footing, a ledge or molding about a foot wide. He almost tumbled off at first, but hung on and struggled for purchase or a grip on a drainpipe or anything he could find, but it was dark back here and the finding was none too easy. Why Mattie hadn't sent him out the same door by which he had come in was perplexing, but he decided that maybe she was just used to shoving lovers out of windows.

Come to think of it, he had bailed out of a few high places himself and survived, and there was nothing to do now but jump. The landing was painful and muddy but he hit, rolled, and was right back up on his feet, albeit limping. Upstairs, the sound of Claude's anger shook the building, but no blows, crying, or gunshots. Jeff listened and was content to limp away, astounded at the things he was having to endure in the name of love, an emotion and state he had always deplored. On top of that it had to be Mattie Silks again, Mattie whose excessive familiarity with what was generally accomplished on mattresses was damned galling if you let yourself think on it—that is, when you had her in your craw as he did.

When Jeff returned, still limping, to where the barber's tent was supposed to be, it wasn't. In fact, all that was left was a three-legged table, three chairs, and a lantern. Playing a desultory game of cards and warming themselves with whiskey were Fatty, Syd, and Yank Hank, bare-chested as usual, and the only one without a blanket around him to ward off the mountain air. Banjo, on the ground, was doing his usual—sleeping.

As Smith came up, Syd pushed the whiskey bottle in his direction.

Fatty answered the question the boss's look demanded: "I rented all my gear from Bob Ford. He foreclosed."

Jeff nodded and took a turn at the bottle. He was cold and a little shaken.

"What do we do now?" Syd asked. The mood was obviously low.

Jeff thought and suddenly seemed to lighten, like a saint on the wall in the grip of an epiphany. "Look tuh Divine intervention!" he told them buoyantly.

Without the faintest idea of what he was talking about, Yank slapped down a card and uttered a fervent: "A-men!"

Chapter Seven

There were two new guards at Ford's toll bridge. Maybe they had heard what had happened to the last two. At least, they appeared a little less aggressive when they were forced to confront an alarming, rumbling, whistling sound from down the trail. They did go on the alert, straining to see through the trees. Suddenly, driving hell-bent toward them and giving no indication of slowing, there came a wagon bearing a steam calliope, the source of the weird whistling.

Holding the reins was a silver-tongued, silver-headed preacher of truly florid mien and wearing a swallowtail coat. A sign on the side identified him as: **THE REVEREND CHARLES O. BOWERS, PASTOR OF PUGILISM.** The guards fingered their weapons nervously, but the wagon came on at the same perilous pace. The Reverend actually laid the whip on the horses.

One of the guards pointed to the sign and shouted: "Toll bridge!"

Bowers only set his jaw and plunged on. The guards had to grab onto the newly installed railings and one of them went farther, throwing himself over the side to dangle.

As he went by, Bowers shouted: "The Lord don't pay tolls!"

When he was past and disappearing in the direction of Creede, the shaken guards pulled themselves together to watch him go, dumbfounded and worrying that they might have to pay Ford the five dollars.

* * * * *

In a copse of trees just outside the town itself, the wagon finally slowed to a stop. Bowers stood on the seat and looked around. Not seeing anyone, he got down and rapped on a side panel of the wagon. A slim man in city clothes emerged, smiling, and paused to brush himself off. With a tip of his derby, he trotted off downhill to disappear among the rocks.

The Reverend Bowers climbed back on the wagon and headed on into Creede, whipping up the horses for his entrance. With the calliope spitting out something that sounded like "After the Ball Is Over" in shrill toots and whistles, he reined in the foaming horses sharply, creating a cloud of dust that blew over many of the idlers lounging in front of Ford's Exchange, who began coughing and slapping at their clothes.

The Reverend jumped down with surprising agility and turned off the calliope. He smiled grandly at the disgruntled loafers and blessed them.

Inside the saloon, he approached the bartender and announced in a booming voice: "I'm here to see Mister Bob Ford."

"He ain't seein'. . . ."

"Don't dally, son. You're standin' in the way of the work of the Lord. Tell him the Reverend Charles O. Bowers is here on a matter of great importance concerning the Almighty Himself."

The bartender was sufficiently impressed by Bowers's bluster and confused by his message that he caved in and went up to Ford's office.

The Rev addressed the remaining bartender: "A little something on the house while I'm waiting, barkeep."

Bat Masterson, idling high in the shotgun's chair, grinned, the only person in the room who suspected what was going on.

Bowers, beaming, was shown into Ford's office by the bartender. The boss, looking morose, sat in his accustomed spot by the window, from where he could survey the street in both directions in case anyone from Missouri should happen to appear there. He had a carbine on his lap and regarded Bowers with a scowl.

"Mister Ford, I understand you're the leading citizen of this lively community. God has blessed you, sir, and what's good enough for the Lord is good enough for me. Now I also understand that . . . may I sit down? . . ."—Ford said nothing, so the Reverend sat without missing a beat —"that the inhabitants hereabouts are as hungry for sporting events as they are for silver and salvation."

"Get to it, preacher," Ford growled.

"I offer a unique opportunity to provide both. You see, I was once a pugilist myself before I gave myself to the Lord. Then I asked myself how can I best use my God-given skill to best serve Him?" He paused to look at the ceiling as if heaven might want to put in a word. "So, in order to gather together the kind of sinners most in need of salvation, so they may hear the Word as preached by yours truly, I promote a full card of prize fighting. The Pastor of Pugilism, that's what they call me."

"A big bag of wind . . . that's what I call you."

Accustomed to skepticism and even hostility, Bowers was undaunted. "A necessary defect of my profession, sir."

He started to stand up in order to use his whole body to theatrical effect, but Ford whipped the rifle around to point at his belly.

"You from Missouri?"

"Absolutely not, sir . . . Indiana! A proud Hoosier. Never have anything to do with those infernal Southerners. The devil's spawn, far as I'm concerned. About the promotion, I'd like to. . . ."

65

"I do all the promoting around here."

"Only natural, sir, but a little bird told me it hadn't been going too well lately. Hard to attract the devotees when they know who's going to win every time. Am I right? Now, it would be unseemly for a man of the cloth to handle wagers. That, sir, would still be entirely your bailiwick. All I would expect is ten percent of the gate and a chance to preach to any of the crowd that wants to remain behind."

Ford gave out a horse-laugh but he was interested, and Bowers could see it or feel it, which is what made him Bowers.

"Not only would a preacher be promoting, but I have a number of novelties with which I salt the card to beguile the crowd. For instance, my friend, have you ever heard of the most extraordinary form of fist fighting in the world, invented by and exclusive to that great nation beyond the seas, France? . . . the manly pursuit of sabot fighting?"

A new sign was promptly hung over the entrance to Ford's Exchange: **BOXING TONIGHT . . . NEW PROMOTER, THE REVEREND CHARLES O. BOWERS, PASTOR OF PUGILISM . . . NOVELTIES AND A FAIR FIGHT PROMISED.** Townspeople, mostly men but a few ladies of bright plumage, were pushing to get in.

Card, roulette, and dice tables were pushed to the side. A fight ring had been set up in the middle of the Exchange's main floor with chairs placed all around it. The crowd filling them was drinking, smoking, spitting, yelling at the fight in progress that was, unfortunately for them, exactly what they'd become accustomed to— Claude Parmenter pounding some hapless challenger into sausage. The loser, a clumsy, outsize miner, was bloody from head to foot but gamely staggered on. Bat Masterson was refereeing. The crowd began to boo.

Ford watched unhappily from the balcony leading to his office. He had Kelly on one side of him and Bowers, smiling down benignly, on the other. That smile irritated Ford.

"What the hell you grinnin' about? Can't you hear all them boos? I thought you'd bring in somebody could put up some fight against Claude."

Kelly groused: "He's been lookin' for 'em all over town like a whore on a blanket with that damn' noisemaker."

"I promised you a crowd, didn't I . . . an' look at it."

"Well, preacher, that crowd's gonna hang you from this balcony if the fights don't improve some."

Bowers leaned over the balcony, studying the scene. "There's some real bruisers down there. We just got to inveigle 'em."

"What about one of your horseshit novelties?" Bob suggested. "Maybe git 'em laughin' anyhow, while Claude beats 'em up."

"Splendid idea, sir." Bowers turned away and trotted down the stairs with his usual alacrity. Ford and Kelly plodded after him.

The most recent opponent was being dragged out of the ring while one of his handlers poured a bucket of water on him. The boos increased and some of the catcalls were getting ugly.

Parmenter preened in his corner and grinned down at Mattie who was sitting nearby with some of her highly decorated girls. She responded with more bile than guile this time.

Bounding into the ring like a much younger man, Bowers held up Claude's hand and announced: "Once again, the winner is Creede's own magnificent pugilist, Claude Parmenter, King of Terrors. Let's have a round of applause for the champ."

More boos. Claude celebrated, oblivious, apparently, of the negative reaction from the crowd, bordering at that moment on hate. Even Mattie couldn't disguise her boredom and she had had a lot of experience faking it.

"Gentlemen, gentlemen, even though an equal combat is a joy to every sporting man, remember that the lion must someday learn to lie down with the lamb and. . . ."

At that point the booing and catcalls began to sound even more dangerous. Someone fired a pistol into the ceiling. Bowers surrendered, holding up his hands. Bat came over to whisper in his ear.

Bowers looked grave and appealed for quiet. It took a while but finally he announced: "Friends, unfortunately it seems that our next challenger has just left town. Is there anyone among you bold gentlemen who would like to match your manly skills with Mister Parmenter?" The crowd went spectacularly silent. "There must be someone with the intestinal fortitude."

"People ignorant enough to fight Parmenter got no intestines left when he gets through," came a voice from the crowd to general applause.

Bowers looked around, found a particularly husky-looking miner, and addressed him: "Sir, what about you? You have the look of a natural-born fighter. What do you say?"

"I say you fight him, big mouth. Just tell us where to send the remains."

He got a certain amount of rough laughter that sounded more like a collective growl than ribaldry. Bowers, whose sense of timing could be counted upon by the fraternity, understood that the moment had come and his eyes scanned the fringes of the crowd.

"I got a challenger here!" someone called out.

Everyone turned to look. Here came Jeff Smith, pushing

into the crowd, behind him Fatty and Yank Hank, escorting the physically modest man that had left Bowers's wagon on the outskirts of town, still in his street clothes. Fatty hefted a bucket of water and Yank had a couple of towels over his forearm like a waiter.

Ford looked on with surprise and anger. He demanded of Kelly how it was that Soapy Smith was in his saloon, not to say in his town?

Kelly shrugged and said: "I thought we run him out. He don't scare easy. If you'd let me settle him. . . ."

Ford pushed his way over to Claude's corner and shouted across the ring at Jeff, who was now in the opponent's corner. "What are you up to, Smith? You got no fighter there."

"I got the only fighter here, Bob. Bugs O'Reilly. Classic match, the elegant fighter ag'inst the slugger." He appealed to the audience who seemed amused by the whole thing and had begun to chant: "Bugs! Bugs!"

Soapy went on: "Y'all want tuh see another fight, don't you, boys? And ladies?" He tipped his hat to a couple of soiled doves sitting nearby, always his greatest champions. "How 'bout it, Bob?" he asked, still playing to the crowd around him. "The Smith bunch ag'inst the Ford gang." His voice rose to a shout as he added—"Winner take Creede!"—and laughed himself at the sheer absurdity of it.

"Let me fight him, boss," Parmenter pleaded with Ford. "I'm not even sweatin'. I'll kill him. That'll be different."

Bowers winked at Ford and turned to Jeff and his party. "All right, sir, bring your Irishman up here and let us get a look at Mister Bugs O'Reilly."

As O'Reilly was helped into the ring by his handlers and began to strip down to his tights, the crowd broke into derisive laughter.

Bowers quickly stepped over to where Ford was standing,

still scowling. "You were right. It's time for novelty. Least-wise, nobody'll know what to expect."

He moved away before the slow-thinking Ford could respond. Returning to the center of the ring and using his megaphone, he explained with the usual filigree that the next fight would be fought in the ancient tradition of gay Paree, sabots, wooden shoes. The rules were different only in the fact that, if either fighter left his shoes, even for an instant, he had lost the fight, no argument.

Jeff's men, Syd, Banjo, and some new gang members, were already moving among the crowd, placing bets on O'Reilly at terrific odds.

Mattie stood, saying loudly to the girls, so that Bob would hear, how she wanted to go place some bets. She had to go around the ring to get to the locus of the betting action and paused briefly to speak to Jeff while pretending to study O'Reilly's singularly spare form. Out of the corner of her mouth, she asked: "You lost your mind, Jeff Smith? Claude's out to kill this joker."

"Bet with me, Mattie, and thank me later."

She gave him a skeptical look. "You mean it?"

He touched his nose and grinned.

Not for the first time did Mattie take a chance on a man.

Chapter Eight

Claude continued to entreat his boss to let him fight, wooden shoes or not. O'Reilly had begun dancing around the ring, punching the air, demonstrating some agility but conspicuously more fragility. Bat came over and advised Ford that it would be unsafe not to let things go ahead.

"C'mon, Bob, what y'all goin' tuh do?" Jeff shouted across the ring so everyone would hear him. "Yuh 'fraid? Put up yuh money . . . I'll bet yuh."

The crowd, half laughing, half still derisive, nevertheless had begun to chant—"Let 'em fight!"—confirming Jeff's experience in other mining towns that any novelty from a goat race to a lynching was hugely welcome among the bored and fatigued. Ford gave the go ahead with a disgusted wave.

The Reverend Bowers just happened to have a pair of sabots in Claude's size, or so he said. Actually they were too large, but Bowers assured Parmenter that this way he would have more freedom of movement. The fighter looked down at the sabots with some amusement but was also puzzled. He took a couple of tentative steps.

"Feel mighty peculiar."

"Just think how they must feel on that skinny Mick," Bowers said. Then leaned closer to whisper: "Carry him for a couple of rounds, Claude."

"That ain't gonna be easy."

"There's actually some people betting on him, so Bob wants it to look good."

71

Over in the other corner Fatty was rubbing grease all over the body of O'Reilly. Yank kept repeating the obvious, that he should avoid being hit at all costs. The fighter nodded perfunctorily, not in the least intimidated.

When Bat called the two fighters into the middle of the ring for their instructions, Bowers joined them. Masterson reinforced the fact that, if either left his sabots, he was the loser, but Claude wasn't much interested.

After the rules had been explained, Parmenter grunted and O'Reilly said: *"Merci."*

"Wha'd he say?" Claude demanded.

"He's begging for mercy," Bowers assured him.

"He won't get none."

Bat sent them to their respective corners and made the *pro forma* announcement. A nod and the bell rang for the first round. Claude clumped out like the giant in a fairy tale, causing Syd to murmur to himself an anxious: "Fee-fi-fo-fum." The big man stopped to look down irritably to see what kind of glue was holding his feet to the canvas.

O'Reilly had shot out of his corner, sabots slapping sharply, and half circled Claude twice, then jabbed him three times from left and right before he knew he was being hit.

When he realized it, he was mildly annoyed and let out an impressive snarl—many previous opponents had quailed before it. But by that time O'Reilly had circled around and was hitting him in the back. These were mosquito bites to a hulk like Claude but he resented them, anyway, as he was intended to. He cast a questioning look at Bowers in his corner—did he really have to carry this irritating little Mick? Actually O'Reilly, while far less robust, was about the same height. Bowers gave Claude a wave of encouragement that made him resigned if not happy. For one thing, the crowd was enjoying the mosquito bites and there were ripples of laughter with every jab. Parmenter was not accustomed to laughter at his expense. He could at least inflict some pain, and he tried a couple of times to hit his opponent where it would hurt, but always the Mick was too fast, dancing on the wooden shoes as if they were ballet slippers while Claude dragged around with hundred pound weights on his feet.

One punch finally caught O'Reilly on the shoulder and he reeled, but the grease saved him, spinning him away like a top from the force of the blow. This unintended maneuver struck the crowd as hilarious, believing as they did that he was making fun of Claude, and they gave him a hand. He paused long enough to bow to them in turn.

Still, the blow had been hard enough to alarm Jeff's gang. Syd came over to where Jeff was sitting and confided: "We got over a thousand bet at grand odds, but if we lose. . . ."

"We won't."

The bell rang and O'Reilly staggered a little getting to his corner where Fatty and Yank were waiting to pour water over him and cover him with more grease. He had a considerable bruise where he had been hit, attesting to Parmenter's power. It was assuaged by a good rubbing with horse liniment. Along with all that and a long sip of the twenty-year-old Bordeaux the fighter had insisted upon, Yank gave him a good pep talk. There was no reason to think that O'Reilly understood a word of it.

"We always get out alive," Soapy was saying down on the floor.

Gentleman Syd continued to fret: "Someday. . . ."

"Look here, when we get to heaven or hell, they'll still have to let us run the games, so what are you worried about?"

In his corner, all Claude wanted to know was: "Now can I kill this god-damn' toe dancer?"

Bowers, answering through the ropes, urged: "Not yet, my

boy. What's the hurry? He can't hurt you."

"You ain't in the ring with him. He's makin' me look like a damn' fool, and it's got me loony."

Mattie, sitting close to Bob and his gang, had begun to catch on and was hard pressed to hide her amusement.

The bell rang again, and this time O'Reilly did a little dance in front of Claude, taunting him. He always stepped away, or sometimes merely leaned back adroitly, when the other reached out beyond his shoes to try to land a blow. Claude began to clump around with more determination, but O'Reilly was back with that jab, catching his opponent on the face a couple of times and leaving red marks. Claude roared and his swings became more furious.

The last straw was when O'Reilly, humming to himself, began a little dance in which he jabbed on every third beat, a-one-and-a-two-bang! He did this while executing a clockwise and then counterclockwise movement around Parmenter, who kept turning clumsily. The crowd took it up and began a chanting cadence. O'Reilly then switched to three-four time, and danced as in a waltz, one-two-three-hit.

The crowd began singing "Casey Would Waltz with the Strawberry Blonde". They were having a wonderful time. Bowers turned to beam at Ford, as if to say: "Isn't this wonderful, a happy crowd?" Ford glowered back, but that was only what The Rev expected.

Driven to new efforts, Claude lunged forward and threw out such a flurry of punches that one was bound to connect. A glancing blow landed, but it was like being kicked by a mid-size mule. Obviously O'Reilly felt the pain and dodged away frantically.

Encouraged, Claude did his lion roar and charged, clomping this way and that by way of trying to cut off O'Reilly. Finally he convinced himself that he had the "damned toe dancer" cornered even though O'Reilly's head bobbed so vigorously it was making him dizzy. He took a mighty swing. O'Reilly ducked low and to the side. Parmenter shot right out of his sabots into the ropes. The crowd exploded into riotous screams of laughter, amazement, and rage. Bat didn't hesitate. He quickly grabbed O'Reilly's arm and raised it high, proclaiming him the winner by virtue of the centuries-old rules of sabot.

Claude, at first stunned, had to be restrained by Fatty, Bat, Yank, and a number of others in the crowd who leaped into the ring, particularly those who had bet against him. Syd and other members of the gang were already out there in the crowd, collecting on their bets.

Ford's boys were yelling at everyone and everything. Ford himself was screaming obscenities across the ring at Smith. Others were too bewildered to know what to do with their rage.

Jeff didn't hesitate. In all that blessed confusion he hustled his fighter out of there. Unnoticed by any of the Ford gang, the Reverend Bowers slipped through the crowd in another direction to escape—something he was very good at—by way of the kitchen. The vicious fights that broke out among the onlookers, particularly the gamblers, only helped him.

Before the inflamed crowd could spill out of the Exchange, the boys came together briefly on the boardwalk in front.

"Almost twenty thousand," Syd announced, showing a wad of bills while looking over his shoulder. "More, but some were reluctant to pay. I figured we can send Fatty and Banjo around when things cool down."

For the first time that evening Jeff beamed. "We're back in business, mah friend. I told yuh."

"If we live," said Syd.

People had begun alternately to storm or drag out now, and not all appeared friendly. "Best we leave the field tuh the vanquished," Jeff said, "who just might be feelin' a mite poorly by now. C'mon, boys, time tuh kick up the heels." He led, hurrying his little army down the street toward the Library.

Inside, Ford was still blessedly occupied arguing with everyone. He knew he had been conned but damned if he could figure out how. Where was that god-damned Reverend? That skinny Mick? And the bastard who had put them all up to it? He began to bellow that he would get revenge on Smith for this, but no one was listening.

So he tried screaming at Claude who was screaming at the imperturbable Masterson. The losers—including some of Ford's own gang—accustomed to betting on Claude despite having to give huge odds were even screaming at Claude, demanding to know who was responsible for letting this happen? Then all eyes and mouths were on Bob Ford.

Ford's answer was: "Where the hell's Soapy Smith? I'll kill that bunghole sniffer. I *willll!*"

The Library had never looked or sounded so festive, the revelers carrying on in such high spirits as to make the onlooking Bob Ford's face resemble an infuriated prune.

"Celebratin' on our money. Makin' fools of us."

"Want us to burn it down?" Kelly asked, hoping.

They were standing in the shadows of some spruce, deep in the shrubbery across the street, watching people come and go. Ford was literally chewing on a nail. The sound of an accordion and fiddle broke out along with the whooping, clapping, and stomping of happy dancers.

"Best whorehouse in town? That'd sure make us popular, Kelly," Ford said.

"She's sold you out, Bob. Gone over to Smith. You gotta do somethin'."

"Where's Parmenter? She's his woman."

"Gettin' drunk, last I saw." Kelly shrugged it off, not having a lot of respect for big muscles when Mr. Colt made all men equal.

"Who else's in there?"

"Some of them city council fellas."

"Those peckerheads!" Bob cursed, and kicked a rock across the street. "They never stood up to nobody."

"I say get the boys together, shoot it up, blow it up, do somethin'."

"You would," Ford said dismally, and stalked away, back toward the Exchange.

If only Ford's men had looked around in back they would have found Jeff and the others. Fatty stood guard, looking around the side of the house. The Rev stood near his wagon.

"Pour toi, mon ami," he said to O'Reilly, who was wearing his sabots, a long heavy coat over his boxing tights, and the derby. Bowers handed him a thick wad of bills. *"Et merci beaucoup."*

"De rien. Merci, merci. Mon plaisir."

Yank appeared, hurrying from in front to tell Jeff: "Ford's yahoos've gone back to the Exchange."

Bowers motioned for O'Reilly to get inside the wagon.

"We-all're real grateful tuh yuh, Rev," Jeff said. "We were in a bad way here."

"Always a pleasure, my boy. When I got your message, I was about to apply the *coup de grâce* to the wastrel son of one of San Francisco's finest families. We were to make a trade, on his part a few of his mother's paltry baubles, on mine most of the western provinces of Canada. Unfortunately I was beaten to the post by a young Jezebel who used the unfair advantage of her sex to sell him the Sandwich Islands."

Jeff laughed heartily. Obviously The Rev owned him when it came to rascally tales. He announced to the others that Bowers was going to hang around and help them harvest the fruits of victory. Calling Fatty over, he told him which way to take O'Reilly out of town, then on to where he could catch a stage. If he couldn't sell the wagon, he might as well dump it in some cañon.

Mattie glided out of the building's back door and came to grip Jeff's elbow and whisper in his ear: "City council wants to meet you."

"An' only yesterday I had leprosy."

The scene inside the Library fulfilled the view that had enraged Bob Ford and his gang—a lot of people having a hell of a good time. The girls were whooping and crying out during dervish whirls of taffeta and crinoline, the miners stepping high like dancing crickets, while the band sawed on. It was only a blind accordionist, two ancient fiddles, and Banjo Parker, but it filled in the few tiny cracks in the blare. Whiskey, beer, champagne, and drinks of every potency and color were being guzzled.

Mattie led Jeff through the hurly-burly to a small group that stood out, even if it hadn't been sitting at a quiet table in a corner, by virtue of their stickpins, stove pipes, and spats.

Jeff muttered—"Aaah, the *bourge-oi-sie*,"—drawling it like a cowhand.

"Gentlemen," Mattie announced as they arrived, "the man who burned Bob Ford's britches on a slow fire, Jeff Smith! Mister Schumhaldter, Mister Cameron, and the head of our city council, Mister Holy Moses."

They stood, and Jeff shook their hands, turning on the famous Soapy charm. With his usual acuity, he knew where the power resided and went right for it. "I bet when yuh struck it big, yuh shouted . . . 'Holy Moses!' . . . loud 'nuff so's they could hear it in Denver." This brought a good chuckle all around.

Moses enthused: "That's right, that's right! Just call me Holy. Most people 'round here do."

"You maybe get only a dollar's worth of silver by shaking hands vith him," Schumhaldter said.

Moses confessed: "If my real name ever got in the papers back East, there'd be a thousand hungry relatives jumpin' higher'n a flea in a cook pan."

Cameron gave Jeff a cigar. Jeff took his time biting off the end and allowing Cameron to light it, encouraging the committee to say their piece.

"Some of us have done all right here, Smith," the ginger-colored Scot said. "Duchie has the freight concession, least till Ford gets around to wantin' it. I got a little mine of my own and a store. Editor of our paper, Cy Warman, he's already impressed with you, but he couldn't be here. He's busy writing up the fight. We're the city council."

"Ve want to stop da killing, get families here," Schumhaldter said.

Jeff shook his head. "Gentlemen, y'all are not a town council." He held up a preëmptory hand as they started to object. " 'Cause yuh don't have a town here, just a bunch uh holes in the ground. An' yuh never will have, long as Bob Ford's runnin' things."

Moses, his folksiness aside, was obviously too shrewd to take offense. "That's mighty plain speaking."

"Bob's 'fraid uh civilization the way a grizzly bear is. Civilization shows up, Bob'll shoot it. Now me, I like a little law,

79

things peaceable so people can have their innocent fun without fear uh harm."

Moses smiled appreciatively. "And you sure ain't afraid of Ford, neither. That's what it'll take."

The others nodded fervent agreement.

Jeff managed to mask his wariness. "What it'll take for what?"

"Bringing in the telegraph," Moses said, his jaw outthrust.

Jeff, for once, was behind the wave. "Well, I dunno now, yuh might just have the wrong fella . . . see, I'm just a gambler and a confidence man."

Cameron led the approval: "By God, how can you not trust a man who says a thing like that?" He clapped Jeff heartily on the back.

Moses said: "We mean to have a telegraph, dammit. I'm worth more than a million just standing here, and I got to wait two, three weeks for a letter from Denver."

"Da company try to bring it in, but Ford, he send night riders out. Tear everything down, burn poles, shoot da vorkers."

"The man who brought in the telegraph," Moses said, "would find plenty hereabouts to thank him."

"And we're not opposed to a little entertainment," Cameron reassured Jeff, "so long as it don't hinder legitimate business."

Jeff looked them over while they awaited his response. "Half the town. Mattie Silks and me get all the entertainment this side of Ford's Exchange. That way he won't feel overly picked on, and you'll get your telegraph. One more thing. Bat Masterson's sheriff."

"Ve already got a sheriff."

"He might be a good man, but he's not a good sheriff. Make him a registrar of deeds, or I'll give him a job."

The other two looked to Moses for his decision. Finally, with a big grin, he extended his hand to Jeff. "You got yourself a deal."

The city council was delighted, and so was Jeff, but he knew better than to let it show. "Calls for some champagne, gentlemen," he suggested, and looked around for a bartender.

"Ah," Cameron uttered suddenly, followed by: "Oh-oh." He happened to be looking past Jeff.

Chapter Nine

Everyone spun to look. Jeff's hand was automatically going for his pistol. Strutting in the door was Claude Parmenter and squeezed under his massive arm, in part holding her up, was a heavily painted, hard-looking night bird. After a couple of steps it was apparent that both were drunk. Their loud voices quickly had a dampening effect on the general gaiety.

Jeff saw Mattie headed for the couple like a red-eyed bull. He stood quickly, excused himself, went off himself to intercept her.

"Hold on, Mattie." He grabbed her arm. "You and him are finished anyway."

"It's my house, Jeff Smith, and I'll say who has a right to come in and shame me in front of my girls."

There was reason to suspect she might have been overlong at the champagne trough herself, but she yanked her arm free, stomped forward, and there wasn't much Jeff could do about it, not being the sort who enjoyed wrestling women in public.

"Mattie," Claude called so everyone would hear as she approached, "this here's Poker Alice! Best lovin' in Creede, by God. Pump all night and get up fresh as a daisy. Also plays a hand of cards tough as any man, so that's another way she might've got her name. Don't you, hon?" He gave her a squeeze and a kiss.

When she came out of it, Alice stepped forward and said: "Hi ya, Mattie. Not a bad little whore . . . house you got . . . here."

Mattie's greeting was to give her a hard right to the jaw, knocking her back against Claude, the only thing that kept her off the floor. It had the effect of sobering her quickly.

Mattie's extension had left her exposed, off balance, and Claude hurled Alice back at her like a blunt instrument. When the women collided, they melded, spun, and toppled to the floor together. By now the whole Library was gathering around, hurrahing the combatants.

Alice was considerably heavier than Mattie. Presently she gained the advantage, rearing up and falling atop Mattie's beautiful silk gown to pummel her. Mattie returned the favor by pulling out handfuls of her opponent's wig and eventually decapitating the wig itself.

Parmenter looked down, grinning, and then around for applause, loving it. He said: "Don't fight girls . . . I ain't worth it," followed by his braying laugh.

Some of the more responsible citizens reached down and pulled them apart. Jeff stepped in to restrain a wildly struggling Mattie.

"What's a matter, Miss Fancy Drawers. Don't you like a good fight?" Alice spat at her.

"I don't like fighting in the dirt with trash." It suddenly registered on Mattie that her gown had been ripped down the front, exposing a lot of leg and some ornate undergarments. She raged about the dress, swearing fervently, and Jeff had to hold on hard.

Abruptly, as if struck by an idea, she stopped her twisting and lunging. Everything stopped with her as the onlookers quieted, puzzled. Slowly, dramatically, Mattie pulled off one of her long white gloves.

Jeff let go of her, thinking she had settled down.

"I demand satisfaction!" she yelled, slapping her opponent across the face with the glove.

The crowd let out an appreciative roar, but Alice didn't get it and sneered: "I know how to give satisfaction, sweetie, but not to you."

That got her a laugh from Claude but it did nothing to stem Mattie's spleen.

"I mean a duel, you rat-haired, cross-eyed, painted-over piss hole."

"Cross-eyed?!" Alice bellowed, and tried to rush at her but was held back by Claude for whom the new idea seemed to hold considerable appeal.

Mattie raised her torn dress high—bringing cheers from the onlookers—to get at her little revolver. Examining the chambers like a professional, she called out for effect: "I challenge you to a duel with pistols, right here and now!"

Jeff was less sanguine. "Mattie, this is goin' too far."

He might as well not have been there. Mattie addressed her audience: "See, she's yellow, won't fight like a lady. I know her. She's one of those nickel-a-night girls from over Denver. . . ."

By now Alice was screaming: "Give me a gun, somebody, gimme a gun!"

Claude was only too eager to comply, handing her his Colt and whispering: "Right 'tween the eyes, darlin'. Settle her good."

"I will. Only"—Alice raised her voice to a shout—"somebody gimme a drink first!"

Several men offered her bottles of whiskey. She seized one and seemed determined to guzzle it all until Claude finally took it away from her. She yelled that it would help her aim but she looked even wobblier than before.

Jeff tried once more to stop it. "Mattie, it's not lady-like to shoot a woman. Anyway, you don't know how."

"Just stay out uh the way, damn you."

"Well, you can't use that little peashooter. Here, take mine." He tried to give her his Colt .45, but she elbowed him out of the way.

"This'll do just fine. All right, everybody!" The room came to a hush. She spotted Bat Masterson in the crowd and called to him: "Count off ten paces, Bat! Then we turn and shoot at will." To Alice she said: "I'll give you the first shot, sweetheart."

"I won't need a second, you round-heeled old biddy."

Mattie was far beyond insults now but had to pause as there were cries from all over to wait until people could get their bets down.

Moses stepped between the girls and announced: "I think this thing's gone far enough. I'm puttin' a stop to it right now."

"You better keep your nose out of it, Holy," Mattie told him, pointing her little pistol in his direction. "You're smack in my line of fire."

A roaring, nasty-tempered demand for violence from the crowd helped convince that civic-minded gentleman to attend the sidelines where he stood, shaking his head disapprovingly.

As the ladies finally worked their way back to back, Masterson slipped up behind Jeff and tried to reassure him that it would turn out all right. Jeff stared at him, wondering about the source of all that confidence. Sometimes you even had to wonder if every male west of the Mississippi hadn't reposed in Mattie Silks's lily-white arms at one time or another. Well, no matter, there weren't many virgins west of that big river, anyway.

Bat moved into the improvised arena to do the count off. "One . . . two . . . three. . . ."

Alice staggered and the crowd held its breath, afraid it was over before it had begun. There were cries of—"She's drunk!"—and—"Hell, no, she's scared!" Someone claimed she had wet her pants and got a laugh even though it wasn't true. It was spilled whiskey.

". . . nine . . . ten."

Alice spun so quickly she nearly fell down. Mattie turned slowly and left her pistol down by her side. Alice seemed to be having trouble seeing her, so the muzzle of her pistol roamed a little.

An anxious Claude stepped up close behind her. "Shoot her, you damn' pickled whore. Settle her, god dammit!"

Alice fired off her round and it went wildly astray. A large number of men and women thought it wise to duck, and their judgment was confirmed when the bullet reached far behind them to shatter a bottle above the bar. Then came roars of laughter, some from relief. The show would go on and their bets were safe for the moment. Alice fired another round that went into the ceiling and knocked down plaster.

"Shoot again, damn you, and hit something," Claude hissed at her. He clearly longed to grab her hand and aim it himself.

But poor Alice was looking bewildered by her lack of success and didn't seem to know what to do next. She studied the gun while Claude rained curses on her from behind. Then she gripped it with both hands and tried aiming again.

Simultaneously Mattie raised her gun and the room went quiet again. She seemed to take deliberate aim while Alice simply gawked at her, no longer able to pull the trigger.

Jeff called out—"Don't Mattie, it's murder!"—but was shouted down. Standing behind, he could almost sight down her barrel as well as she. Perfect aim, straight at Alice's head, while everyone held their breath and Holy Moses turned away. But then Jeff was startled to see Mattie shift her aim slightly to the left.

The crack of the .25 seemed so much louder than it was, for another silence—this one absolute—dropped like a heavy weight on the room and clung for several seconds. There was the sound of a slight moan and then of a tree falling to the wooden floor as Claude Parmenter, King of Terrors, toppled, a reddening hole between his eyes.

"Oops," Mattie said quietly but was heard everywhere, "I missed."

The silence was shattered by a roar. Alice looked down at Claude and immediately passed out next to him. For the moment they were ignored amid the loud quarreling over what to do about the bets.

Cameron finally checked on Parmenter and announced: "Right through the brain, if he'd had one."

Gentleman Syd, looking on, said: "The poor bastard drew deuces twice in the same day."

No one seemed to care much except for a lone mourner who appeared suddenly and let out a loud wail, falling across the body before anyone could haul him away. "Oh, Claude, my dear ol' pal," Yank Hank sobbed, clutching the lapels of the corpse's plaid jacket and burying his head in his chest.

Most of the crowd was still in argument or had gone back to carousing, but Jeff and Syd looked at their companion with a dark skepticism. "What the hell?" Jeff said.

Syd went over and helped some do-gooders, Moses among them, pull the grief-stricken Yank Hank off the body as a crowd gathered around this new excitement. Syd had to hold him up to keep him from collapsing in his *extremis*.

Jeff came over and studied Parmenter while some men hefted him up, prepared to take him to the undertaker. The boxer's shirtfront was torn. Smith touched it, grinned, and went to catch up with Syd and poor Yank Hank as they headed for the back door.

"He takin' yuh off tuh the lunatic asylum?" he asked, gripping Fewclothes's other arm.

"Claw Pawmtur wa ma fran'. Goo' ni'!"

Yank Hank tried to scramble loose, but Jeff slapped him sharply on the back and a large diamond stickpin became a projectile headed for the floor. One second after it hit, Yank Hank was on his knees, grabbing for it, and two seconds after that he was fleeing for the door with it clutched in his hand, still shouting, although with better elocution, that Claude was still his beloved friend.

Jeff went back to where Mattie was graciously accepting congratulations on her poor marksmanship from an admiring group of miners and soiled doves.

He pulled her aside and murmured: "Where'd you learn to shoot?"

"Wyatt, in Denver. First solid man I ever lost that way, though." She gave him a telling look. "By accident."

"I certainly hope it's the last," he said with a wan smile. Then, thinking about it: "Wyatt Earp? How old are you, Mattie?"

She stepped away, looked at him over her shoulder with a smile that could kill a large quadruped, and sashayed back to the bar where an audience of admirers awaited. They hoisted her atop the bar where she sat, leaning forward, her exposed legs crossed. They urged her either to sing a song or to tell them again how she had "accidentally" dealt with the man who had done her wrong.

Chapter Ten

Two days later Jeff sent his gang, such as it was, out of town, scattering in different directions. It was remarked upon and yet no one knew where they had gone or what they were up to. Even the urbane Bowers went out, although on a mule as he couldn't abide horses.

Ford's interest was concentrated on Jeff. He was sufficiently cunning to know who had the key to everything that was causing him trouble. Smith was staying at the Royal Hotel, catty-cornered across the street from the Exchange.

"Here he comes," Lev said, posted in the window of the office. "Got saddlebags with him."

Ford, Kelly, Pony Bill, and another cowboy named Cale, a tobacco chewer with a droopy mustache, moved quickly to the window.

"Headed for the livery stable," Pony Bill noted with his genius for the obvious.

"Seein' as how they went ever' which way yesterday when Cale followed," Lev said, "I 'spect they're gettin' while the gettin's good."

"They're not leavin'," Ford told them, and no one argued.

Cale said: "Had I made me as much on that prize fight as they did, sure as Hades I'd go where the spendin' was more fun."

"I'd sure like to get those winnin's back," Kelly muttered.

"They ain't goin' nowhere," Bob Ford repeated. "I've got people to tell me things. Ol' Holy Moses gave Smith an earful 'bout bringin' in the god-damn' telegraph."

"Been others tried that, Bob," Kelly said with a certain pride. "But I still say . . . the sure way to best Soapy Smith's to fill his mouth with dirt."

"And I told you how I feel about that."

"There ain't no telegraph that don't reach Missoura, Bob."

Ford had to think about that, always hard work, but first indecision and then decision played out on his face while the others watched the struggle intently and waited impatiently.

"Go down and kill him."

"Right here in town?" Lev asked, pleased but surprised.

"No, you damn' fool. But not too far out of it, either. Just don't leave nothin' behind that comes back on me, you understand?"

"Might just have some of them winnin's in them bags," Kelly observed.

"He does, they're all yours, boys."

That brought a lot of *whooees* and *ah-has* as the "boys" scrambled to be first after their prey.

Jeff was riding easily about a mile south of town on the downslope to the flatlands that stretched to the New Mexico border. It was here that through the pines he became aware of several hoof beats behind him, clopping, walking, their sounds echoing off the cañon walls.

To a man of Smith's experience, this could not be an innocent occurrence. He decided to pick up speed, raising the horse to a trot. Listening keenly, the party behind him was soon doing the same. Was this some kind of mockery? He went on at the same pace for a while. If somebody was playing with him, he wanted to use their own game to escape from the trap presented by the narrow defile.

He decided after a while to take it up to a canter, and the horses behind did the same. It had become predictable, yet they failed to come on and make a real try for him. It was Ford's men back there. He had no doubts by now. They might be funning him at the moment, adding a little torment for the money they had lost, but it was only the start of something.

This was perfect set-up for them, Jeff reasoned. Ford probably wouldn't want it known that he was responsible for his rival's death lest it bring a dangerous notoriety, but here Jeff would be just a hole in the meadow and the world wasn't apt to miss one more grifter or gambler. No, they were out to kill him. He should have stayed in town.

He went across Ford's bridge at a full gallop, rattling the posts and planks. The two guards were confused at first, but just when they got ready to shoot at his disappearing back, here came six more at the same dangerous speed, screaming wild cries from the saddle. The guards didn't have time to register them as Ford's men. The riders were a blur, a whirlwind of motion and black thunder on the boards. One of the guards was knocked into the water and the other just managed to cling to the side, half on and half off.

Jeff was riding for his life now. He caught sight of the meadow with its shrubbery, tall grass, and flowers just ahead, but suspected he would never get there without some help. He jettisoned the saddlebags.

When Kelly's band caught sight of them, to a man they pulled up hard on the reins. Pony Bill was first to reach the saddlebags, but Cale wasn't having any of that and, without a word, hit him on the jaw, knocking him down. With a victorious yell, Cale grabbed up the saddlebags for himself. Yet before he could rip them open, Pony Bill had him by both legs, dragging him to earth where they rolled one way and then the other, pounding on each other.

Lev and two other cowboys were so delighted by the show they forgot why they were there. Kelly reminded them by firing a few shots into the ground inches from their feet. They jumped in to help him kick and drag the two combatants apart, cursing them to heaven for the worst fools ever to sit a saddle.

"We're here to kill Soapy Smith, god-damn you to perdition," Kelly cursed. "What's in those bags, anyhow? Better be lots of silver, after this." Grabbing them up off the ground himself, he ripped one open, then the other, and his face instantly reddened. He bellowed furiously: "Jerky and long johns! That's what you donkeys were makin' damn' fools of yourself over." He began yanking out the items and throwing them all over the landscape. "He'll die slow, the bastard. Sure as there's a God Almighty I'll stake him out and ride over him."

Finally, exhausted by his own passion, he looked around for a moment and it dawned on him that they had given their quarry a good jump ahead. "Get in your saddles, you goddamn' bohunks, an' earn your pay."

If they were riding fast before, it was an inferno of speed now, trying to make up for lost time, screaming continuously while bringing blood with their spurs.

Jeff was riding flat-out across the meadow. He had spotted a sunken stream ahead that seemed to offer the only cover within reach and made for it, hoping to drop out of sight. Finding a natural ramp down, he took the horse to water and jumped off himself to dampen his face and rest for a few minutes. He had been a Texas waddie in his youth but for years his natural habitat had been smoke-filled rooms.

He was beginning to hope he might have lost his pursuers when a tiny geyser of water erupted right in front of him. The sound of the shot had been too far away to notice.

Creeping up to the rim of the cut, he searched the landscape. Tiny puffs of smoke located the shots for him, and there were more of them now, whizzing into the turf close by. They were coming from several rifles and carbines up on the last ridgeline before the descent into the valley.

He slid back down until his boots were in the mud, pulling his pistol from the holster and then realizing the futility of that. Hunkering in the streambed had seemed like a good idea, the only idea at the time, but it had resulted in his being trapped. He huddled against the bank, trying to think his way out, listening to the shots going overhead.

If they couldn't hit him, or the horse—and so far that didn't seem to have occurred to them—they would eventually come down, encircle him, and the only place you would find Soapy Smith thereafter would be in a dime novel.

Suddenly the shooting stopped. Jeff scrambled up again to look. No sign of gunfire from the ridge. He knew what that meant: they were coming down after him. There was no going back the way he had come down. He would be on the wrong side of the creek with no guarantee of getting across. Wiping the sweat out of his eyes, he ducked low and ran along the creekbed to catch up with his horse as it wandered along, eating the long grass served by the water.

His heart was pounding now as it never would have in a saloon shoot-out. He heaved himself up into the saddle. The horse, startled, shied, and threw him, injuring his right shoulder. He wasn't sure if it was broken, out of joint, or just hurt like hell. But there was no question of staying on the ground indulging it. In seconds he was back up, stroking and murmuring soothing words to gentle the beast.

In his second attempt he remained in the saddle, although it took a moment to settle the animal down. At last he could bend low across the pommel and urge the horse along the creekbed in search of a ramp or even a low dip in the cut that would get them out on the other side.

A couple of rounds flew well over his head. Contrasting it with the previous shooting, he thought this probably came from the saddle. Gross inaccuracy only meant they were riding fast in his direction with the blood running high. He tried a way up. The horse, *el presidente*'s white stallion, César, didn't make it on the first try, slipping back, legs flailing, all akimbo, rearing his head side-to-side and whinnying with fear. Jeff was more sentimental about horses than most ex-cowboys, but this was *his* life or death. He clutched the reins hard and fought César, dug in his spurs ruthlessly in the effort to get him headed up again.

It was a frantic, messy scramble with the horse's hoofs making sucking and slipping sounds in the muck, Jeff's fervid voice alternately threatening and begging him. Somehow they made it, but once on level ground they froze for a few seconds while skylined there on the bank, inanimate as a monument in a park, both horse and rider apparently surprised by their success and paralyzed by the effort. It was a fatal moment.

Before thought came back to Jeff's mind, several shots—he could hear them plain enough now—were fired from not far away, still fired from the saddle but with a much more substantial target. One of the rounds went straight into the horse's brain. His head shivered, raised slightly before he went down like a ship capsizing, toppling on his side, eerily without excess movement or sound.

Jeff tried to throw himself free but still one boot caught under the thousand pound *corpus*. His foot was in that boot. For a moment he thought it was hopeless, but then, stretching his upper body and looking around desperately, he found a dead tree branch on the ground just above where his head lay, almost touching his hair. Grabbing it, he managed to maneuver it under the horse's still quivering body and, using a flat rock that was already in place for a fulcrum, levered his foot out from under. The boot remained.

There was no time for celebration or pain. In seconds he was on his hands and knees and crawling, throwing himself ahead into the high grass with arms and legs flapping like a berserk turtle's. He wanted to get down as deeply into the scrub and as far from the horse as possible before they rode up. He could already hear their coming, the horses pounding the earth and the insensate yelling.

When it seemed they must be at the side of the stream, he moved slowly, then came a stop, drew his pistol, and stopped breathing, listening intently. Kelly led the others arriving at the creek. His mount, foaming, reared at the cusp. When he got it under control, he stood in the stirrups and shaded his eyes, studying the dead horse on the other side and the landscape beyond. To the others, as they rode up, their horses also lathered and panting, he shouted: "Where is he? Where in the hell is the bastard? I don't see him nowheres."

"How do he get across?" Pony Bill asked.

"Jes-us, my horse's smarter than you. Spread out and find where he did it."

The gang began to range up and down the creekbank, looking for the same path down that had served Jeff.

"I think we got him, Kelly," Lev said, following his stare. "I saw him go down."

"You don't see him over there, do you?"

"I know we hit him," Cale said. "I saw him get hit."

A victory cry went up from one of the men, drawing the other riders to him and on down into the creekbed. All they had to do, then, was look at Jeff's horse to find their way onto the other bank.

"Find him!" Kelly shouted. "Ride him down if he's out there somewheres." He waved his hand over the meadow like Merlin laying a curse on the land.

The high country sun was climbing toward noon. It was getting hot out on the flat land. The vegetation offered Jeff some cover, but the heat combined with fear brought sweat running from every pore. He couldn't risk even the minimal movement needed to wipe it away. It was possible to hear every word, they were that close. Every time they started to talk among themselves, he would use their distraction and noise to dare a little crawl in this direction or that.

If they discovered him, the best he could hope for would be taking down one or two, and then a quick death. He had one real hope. Hired shooters went soft in the towns. No one in this bunch would have the slightest tolerance for anything that resembled work or discomfort.

Still, the tramping of horses drew closer, both in front and around him. He would try to gauge a rider's position and zig or zag away from it, not even on his hands and knees now but slithering the best he could with his injured shoulder and holding his Colt at the instant ready.

Once he saw the legs of a horse, for a few seconds his heart stopped, knowing that any movement on his part, even of the lungs, might prove fatal. He tried to flatten himself to the earth while rolled into a ball like a hedgehog. The horse's breathing, whinnying, then the rider's unhappy grunts came closer.

Suddenly the man spoke and it seemed like near thunder in Jeff's ears. "Must of crawled into a hole to die," Pony Bill drawled. But he went on by, five or six feet from Jeff's head, silver jingling, humming "Rose of Tralee" under his breath. His prey was finally able to take life back into his tortured body, but softly even though he longed to gasp.

The sounds of tramping horses went on all around Jeff, but he clung to the earth with the determination of a man who wasn't ready to enter it. Voices boomed and retreated.

"We got him, Kelly," Lev said. "You know we did." He sounded bored.

"We sure as hell didn't git that money." Cale was beginning to feel sorry for himself.

Another member of the posse, a voice not recognized by Jeff, put in his two cents: "An' it's hot enough out here to roast a goat."

Pony Bill had a popular idea. "I say we kilt him dead and ol' Bob ought to pay us extra for what we didn't get for it."

That brought some laughter and several voices raised to register agreement.

Lev chimed in: "Prob'ly out in all that grass dyin' right now."

"Likely crawled in some hole to die," someone else said.

Kelly wasn't so sure, but his troop's morale seemed to be on the wane, and finally he accepted the rationalization. They rode back the way they had come, fast and filling the heavy air with victorious whoops.

Jeff rolled over onto his back, crammed the pistol in its holster, and checked to see that he was still wearing his money belt. True, he had lost a favorite horse, but the silver was still there. Only then did he let it all out in one giant, prolonged exhalation.

Smiling, he reached up and plucked a wildflower, held it to his nose, and sucked in the odor. So good to be alive—even with one boot, no food or blanket, and a long, long walk ahead. All it meant was just one more time that he would have to "ride into the sunset and come out at dawn full of piss and vinegar".

Chapter Eleven

Nothing was seen of Jeff or his friends for a couple of weeks, and the general opinion was that they would never return. A few were made very happy by that view, but more were disappointed and even a little sad. Of course, the vast majority didn't care about much of anything except dreams of silver and the saturnalia it could buy.

Rumor spread that Bob Ford's gang had killed Jeff a few miles outside of town and that did worry his friends. Ford began to overcome his own suspicions, not to say parsimony, and believed the rumors to the extent of rewarding the posse members lavishly for their success. He had his town back. In time he intended to rid himself of Mattie Silks and that perfidious, self-appointed city council.

However, this *bellum interruptum* was not to last. A few days after Ford had settled with the posse members an old wagon pulled into town and stopped in front of the Library. Atop it were the Reverend Bowers and Yank Hank Fewclothes, in the back, Banjo Parker, dozing. Not that they were easily identifiable as such. The Rev, usually so presentable, was dressed as a teamster down on his luck and with a full beard. Yank had actually put on a shirt, swallowtail coat, coonskin hat, and wore a mustache. Banjo always looked shabby and he was too big to care.

They unloaded some boxes and hefted them inside, the girls crowding the windows to watch and wonder, and from across the street the town loafers. Soon Yank was out on the porch, nailing up a sign—**CREEDE TELEGRAPH OFFICE**—and beneath it in more modest printing: **Smith & Co**.

One of the loafers called over to him: "Say, you really mean it?"

"Naw," Yank told him, "I'm only doing this 'cause I lost a bet."

Another porch sitter called: "First I ever heerd of a telegraph in a sportin' house!"

"Why not? More of you pass through here than any other building in town."

Bowers appeared in one of the downstairs windows and passed Yank a wire, both of them too busy to hear the *clanking* spurs or wonder what had happened to turn the loafers and girls silent. When Yank looked up, he found Lev, Cale, and Pony Bill on foot, staring at him from the street and spitting in the dust.

"Whatya think yer doin', crowbait?"

The Rev saw them, tipped his hat politely, and quickly disappeared back into the house, leaving his confederate standing there, holding a wire in one hand and a telegraph key in the other.

"I don't believe I've had the pleasure, sir," Yank said grandly, and went back to work.

"Don't give me none of that fancy hogwash," Lev said. "I know you for one of the late Soapy Smith's men . . . the loon that goes 'round half-naked."

Yank tried to ignore him, hooking up the key, and putting it on a table.

"Busy as a biscuit, ain't he?" Pony Bill said.

Lev addressed Yank again: "You must be touched. There ain't no wire for a hundred miles 'round."

Cale said: "Ain't no Soapy Smith gonna bring it, neither. He's wearin' horns an' a tail by now."

"Maybe we oughta go tell Bob," Pony Bill said. "Give him a humorous feelin'."

Lev looked at him darkly and in a quieter, less confident, tone said: "You think so, do you. Well, c'mon, you tell him."

One of Ford's bridge guards was standing, leaning on one of those newly installed railings, picking his teeth and watching the turbulent water below with no outward sign of cognitive activity. Suddenly some furious activity assaulted his dull mind. A dinghy with three men, all stripped to the waist, raced across the white water in his direction—Jeff, Fatty, and Syd, soaked and happy.

The other guard quickly joined him to ask, slack-jawed: "Do we charge 'em?"

As the dinghy passed under the bridge, they could see a windlass on the stern playing out some kind of wire or cable. The two guards dashed to the other side of the bridge to see the boat come out. The three occupants waved cheerfully, and the boys on the bridge, passably confused, waved back. The boat darted out of view around a bend.

"I guess not."

Not long after this episode at the bridge, a young boy raced into the Bonanza Saloon and informed Holy Moses, standing, drinking, and jawing at the bar with some of the respectable element, that great events were occurring down at Wolf Creek. The whole bar emptied, the men knocking each other out of the way when they saw Moses and the others hurrying somewhere. Maybe it was another big strike.

Jeff knew, among other things, how to put on a show. He had one man plowing a deep furrow with an ox team that ran from the creek into town as far as the Library. Two were carrying the windlass behind the plow, stringing wire along the bottom, while still others followed them and covered it with dirt. The diggers had all been employed for the job as none of Jeff's gang was wont to be seen with a shovel in his hands.

Most of the town came, including several barking dogs, one of which kept trying to bite the wire and had to be shooed away over and over again. Jeff, Syd, and Fatty, putting on their shirts, straightened and brushed their clothes, and then led the small parade to the Library.

Everyone wanted to shake their hands, although most of the crowd didn't have the least notion why. They were just excited by . . . something. Jeff answered greetings by calling to people by name, one of his skills. The celebration resembled that of returning exiles after a successful revolution. For Jeff it was only a performance, one he enjoyed, but still a performance. From his point of view the citizenry cheered you one minute and were just as happy to see you waltzing on nothing the next. He was a man without the illusions that for most of us make life bearable.

He did feel something when he saw Mattie on the porch, waving her lace handkerchief at him, one he had given her in Denver. It got even better when she threw off her usual armored control to run down off the porch and throw her arms around him, kissing him wildly to general hilarity and applause.

Jeff finally broke it off: "Hold on, honey. These yahoos here never seen nothin' like this. Yuh want tuh scandalize all uh Creede?"

Oh, how the crowd loved it.

Also waiting on the porch were several of Mattie's girls, Bowers, back in his usual sartorial splendor, Yank Hank without his shirt, and Banjo Parker, sleeping on the swing behind them, playing no part in anything. Moses and some of the swells were so eager to join it was soon a very crowded porch.

Jeff trotted the last few steps to the house and leaped up on the porch to join them, Syd coming to stand by his side. Fatty joined up with Bowers, and the two of them went into the house.

"You sayin' this thing's gonna work, Soapy?" one rough-hewn type called out.

Jeff remained pleasant and statesman-like. "I told yuh I'd bring it here, an' now I'm telling yuh it's goin' tuh work."

Moses threw in—"Then you got yourself a deal."—and a lot of people cheered, again without the slightest idea of what he was talking about. Jeff shook his hand and someone took a photograph.

Over his shoulder Jeff called out to Yank, loud enough to be heard across town: "Ready Mister Telegrapher?"

Yank, still seemingly fiddling with the equipment, called back: "Nearly so, Mister Smith!"

"Well, hurry it up. Creede's been waitin' a long time for a chew on the T-bone uh progress."

Yank rubbed his hands together as if he were going to roll some dice, took a deep breath, and tapped out some signals. Nothing came back. *Tap-tap-tap* came again. No answer.

A discontented hush settled over the crowd and even those on the porch. Only Jeff Smith seemed unconcerned. Yank held his hands above the key as if praying to the god of communication. Now people stirred. Moses gave Smith an anxious glance that he shrugged off. He held up a hand, urging patience. Suddenly the key began to *clatter* by itself.

A huge cheer went up, but Yank cut it short by waving for quiet so he could hear. Jeff pushed his way in beside him and grabbed the message pad away from Yank before he had finished writing.

In stentorian tones Jeff said: "Ladies and gentlemen. Creede's just joined the modern world. Here's our first message! 'What hath God wrought?' Western Union, Denver."

More cheers drowned out the last few words but no one cared, least of all Soapy Smith, who was trying to survive an army of strong-armed people trying to pound him on the back or shoulders and a lot of the girls kissing him anywhere they could find.

When he could get free, he announced: "Folks, the Smith and Company Telegraph office is now open. Line forms to the right."

The scramble began, an unruly mob of lonely men fighting for a place in a line that would eventually stretch right out of town.

Syd kept the fire under it. "Step right on over, boys and girls, a dollar a word to send off, a mere half dollar to receive. Send a message to your loved ones . . . or to someone you hate . . . costs the same. Now, in honor of the pioneer who made all this possible, the first message to be sent will be by our very own president, Randolph Jefferson Smith himself."

A friendly voice from the crowd asked: "Who's it to, Soapy?"

And another—"Maybe he don't wanna say."—got a few hoots.

There was a lot of curiosity about this, especially from Mattie, who even appeared a bit anxious. Jeff simply looked modest and sincere—faking sincerity was so much a part of his life that he couldn't forego it even when he was telling the truth. "Tell the God's honest truth, boys, it's been mah life-long habit tuh send some kind uh message tuh mah mother in Texas ever' Saturday night."

There was a lot of good-natured raillery at this, but Mattie turned on one of her sisters-in-love sharply. "Quit braying like a donkey . . . it's true. Jeff comes from fine Georgia people who moved to Texas after the war. His father was a lawyer who died of the drink when he was a boy." A certain regret entered her voice. "I think sometimes his mother's the only person he's ever really loved."

Out on the street a different atmosphere began to simmer with enough ions in the air to presage a coming storm, which was the case.

"Bob Ford's come out," someone said, and the news rippled through the crowd faster than Smith's telegraph.

Bob and his men—Kelly, Lev, and a half dozen others—all mounted and cussed-looking as they could manage, moved relentlessly toward the Library with a hostile glare for everyone. Some of the crowd began to slip away, others simply pulled back to open the stage and leave it accessible to the real players.

Mattie clutched Jeff's arm while he exchanged looks with Holy. "I'm just a sharper. It's time somebody respectable stood up for this town, don't yuh think?"

Moses nodded. "We'll back your play."

Everybody was eyeing everybody else by the time the Ford gang pushed their way onto the scene. Cameron and a couple of the "respectables" stepped down after Holy, if with less enthusiasm.

"What do you want, boys?" Holy asked.

"You know," Ford said. He always wore an overly large hat when he came out into the open air that served to hide his ever-shifting eyes, always looking for the first place where someone might jerk a gun on him. "That pack a slickers and buncos better get out of this town."

Suddenly Jeff stepped off the porch and strolled past Holy Moses, smiling, hand extended to Ford. His voice was theatrically loud. "Say, Bob, now yuh're out in the sunshine, how 'bout us two sittin' down an' talkin' this over like gentlemen."

He never got very close because Kelly drew his pistol with impressive dexterity and fired four rapid shots in a squared pattern at the ground around Jeff's feet. If the idea was to frighten him, make him dance perhaps, it failed. Jeff simply looked down at the dust where the rounds had struck, raising tiny clouds. The citizens nearest him were less sanguine and leaped back in a hurry.

Jeff shook his head as if disappointed. "That's not a bit friendly." Inclining his head slightly and raising his voice, he shouted: "Don't kill 'im 'less yuh have tuh, Fatty! But if he does that ag'in, give him both barrels."

In a room upstairs in the Library—one with a sign on the outside of the door that said: **If You Want To Die, Come On In**—Fatty, nowhere near the window, was picking up a couple of cards off a table with one hand and drinking beer out of a pitcher with the other. "Hey," he said, puzzled, to Bowers who had dealt him the card, "you hear Soapy call me?"

"Play," The Rev grumbled.

Down on the street, Holy Moses looked Bob Ford right in his shaded, squinting eyes and said: "The city council, the voice of the people of this town, says they stay."

Ford hadn't expected that and for a moment remained indecisive. He looked around at the crowd of miners, teamsters, laborers, drifters, and all he saw were hostile eyes, set mouths, and concrete jaws. In a tone that was almost an appeal he said: "They're thieves. They'll skin you alive."

Jeff said—"No more'n is fair."—and got a nervous laugh from the bystanders.

Kelly put his gun back in its holster but kept his hand on the butt. Syd and Banjo now came down to stand beside Jeff. It was eight to three, but the crowd behind them, including several of the fair Cypriots cheering him on from the upstairs windows, was clearly backing Jeff and his telegraph.

After a twitchy few minutes in which one could have heard a locust breathe, the gang began to back up their mounts, turn them, and move slowly away, trying to salvage some dignity.

From one of the upstairs windows, Fatty's voice yelled down: "Say, Soapy, did you call me?" He couldn't figure out why that got a huge laugh from the crowd and looked perplexed.

Jeff waved him away disgustedly.

Moses called after the departing cowboys: "Jeff gets this end of town! You keep everything north of the Exchange. Plenty here for both of you."

The miners cheered, but Kelly was angry enough with his boss to jerk back on the reins and make his horse rear. "You givin' in, Bob? They'll have the only good whorehouse. It's a god-damned crime. I ain't takin' it from them."

"Kelly," Ford said sternly, "come along." He signaled for the troop to follow him. He did get in a last word, or thought he did. "Every dog has his day." With that he continued on up the street toward the Exchange.

Ford wasn't looking back when Yank ran out into the street to hand Jeff a telegram that made him laugh when he read it. He boomed to the crowd, making certain that Ford could still hear him: " 'Congratulations, Jeff Smith, on bringing the telegraph to Creede.' " Then his voice rose to a real shout: "Signed . . . Frank James!"

Ford whirled in his saddle, his whole countenance jumping and twitching with alarm while his hand grabbed the pistol on his hip, until he realized that the crowd was roaring with laughter—at him. With a dog-like snarl he dug the spurs into his pinto and rode hard to get to the other end of town, away from that flaying sound. The gang followed in some disarray.

Chapter Twelve

Jeff's flame had never burned brighter than it did in the weeks
following the coming of the telegraph and facing down Ford's
gang. A stock exchange was made possible by the wire to
Denver, owned and managed, of course, by Smith & Co.
Thanks to the help of the newly empowered city council that
had suddenly discovered a dire need for fire and safety laws,
Jeff bought out two saloons south of the new borderline, setting himself up in the largest. With a lot of revamping, it became the Tivoli, named after one he had owned in Denver. It
was advertised as the finest establishment of its kind between
San Francisco and St. Louis.

From there, while standing at the bar, Jeff preached
peace and prosperity based on civic duty, law and order,
and the paying of debts when called. Over the entrance was
a sign writ large: **THE WAY OF THE
TRANSGRESSOR IS HARD**—and below that in considerably smaller print— **... to change**. Jeff said this wise
saying had been laid down by the Roman lawyer, Cicero.
Bat became sheriff, mostly south of the new border, but
didn't have much more to do than buffaloing drunks.
Trade and entertainment thrived in south Creede now that
it was civilized. Traveling bands and theater troops added
the city to their circuit; opera singers were always welcome.
Out on the street fire-eaters and dancing bears attracted
people to the Tivoli.

Smith, in his customary *faux* modest manner, demurred

and gave all the credit to the new city council that sang his praises in return. He stuck to his black suits and hat, but did take to carrying a cane and wearing a foulard and stickpin.

Jeff saw the pickings as so good he sent for more members of his old gang. He was confident he could control them. Others, tolerated but not sought, were drawn by the rumors. Everyone followed the rules and tithed to Jeff and his inner circle, or left town in worse shape than they arrived.

The famous Canada Bill stopped by for some sociability while plying his trademark three-card monte, as usual making his way by keeping things simple. There was Doc Baggs, inventor of the "gold brick", Judge Van Horne, disbarred, Ice Box Murphy, who had once blown one, thinking it was a safe, and Frisco Red Harris. The Great Gobblefish, Eat-'Em-Up Jake Cohen, and Yeah Mow Hopkins also arrived. This last was a brutish Caucasian who had been a hatchet man for the San Francisco tongs and even wore his hair in a cue. Some said he had been around the Chinese so long he looked like one, although in truth he was pale, outsized, and had been born in Minnesota. Many of the others chose to stay away from him, but Jeff found he had his uses.

One day Mattie stormed into Jeff's office where he was eating lunch and reading several newspapers at once, having always been a demon for papers and reading in general. Both knew this was his private time and that he guarded it zealously. Mattie was so upset and fulminating that Jeff had trouble understanding what it was all about and got a little impatient, which did nothing to improve her temper. It had something to do with a girl named Creede Lily who appeared to have been beaten, a not unknown phenomenon in the marginal world so long as it didn't go too far. Sometimes the beaten came back and shot or stabbed the beater, and

108

that was generally forgiven, too.

"Creede Lily? One uh yuhr girls? I don't place her."

At this point Mattie began to rail at him for being an "uncaring baboon" and even less charitable descriptions. Considering that Creede was a ways from being a nunnery, Jeff was accustomed to overly agitated women and usually took them in stride. He called for Syd to come and remove Mattie so he could get some peace and quiet.

Syd struggled manfully to drag her out while Jeff suggested: "Offer her somethin' she can't refuse . . . laudanum, morphine, a pipe. Hell, ennathin', I don't care, but git her out uh here!" After that Mattie went easier, with opium dreams already shading her eyes.

Cy Warman, the publisher of the *Creede Candle*, came in, passing Syd and Mattie going out and shaking his head at Mattie's overwrought appearance. "You tell him, Cy," she said as she went.

Warman laughed. "That is surely a passionate woman. And she does care for her girls."

The publisher and Jeff had become friendly of late, and Smith was always available to the press. "I couldn't make hide nor hair uh what she was sayin', she was goin' on so. Sit down, Cy, always pleased tuh have yuh." He offered him a drink but Warman declined.

"I'm here on the same errand as Mattie, I'm afraid . . . this Creede Lily thing that happened. I don't know if you want to hear or not."

"Never know till yuh try."

Cy pulled his chair closer to Jeff's desk and lowered his voice just a bit. "I've gotten to see a lot of you in these last few weeks, Jeff, and I've liked what I've seen. But truth is, I don't really know you. Your reputation from other places is that you're a man with a conscience, particularly where the weak and pitiable are concerned. On the other hand, I have no doubt you can be . . . well, pretty tough where your own interests are concerned. But in Creede, I'd say any judgment calls for a little relativity."

"Good word . . . I like it."

"I can see where you would," Warman said, and broke into a grin.

"I hope I'm that fella yuh described. But damned if yuh aren't soundin' more like a preacher than a newspaperman, Cy."

Warman stayed serious. "Maybe so. You haven't seen the girl. She won't be working in this business again."

On the way over to the home of the elderly widow who had taken Lily in and was caring for her, walking swiftly, Warman explained to Jeff: "I would have had the bastard arrested, but I didn't think he should get off with a fine, which is the way it's been around here. And, then, some of the boys idling around were acting a mite ugly and I didn't want to see another lynching, either. Anyway, it's your town, or soon will be."

"Who is he?"

"Some low life from over in Utah who got real big for his britches. Well, he is big. Calls himself Salt Lake Billy Thompson, I think."

"What's he do?"

"Everything, I guess. Claims to be a *pistolero,* but this trouble started when he tried to add Lily to a string of girls he takes around."

Jeff spat—and he rarely spat—when he heard that.

Looking down at the comatose Creede Lily, lying moaning on a settee with the widow sniffling in the background, Jeff was reported by Warman to have bitten his lip. Some felt an unknown stratum of emotion must somehow have been mined in Jeff Smith, but she truly was unrecognizable, never again to have a face that was any part of anyone's fortune and would have dismayed even a mortician.

"Sweet-natured girl . . . now I know her," Smith said gently. But then, aroused suddenly, he shouted: "Where's that no-good doctor? Has he seen this poor little thing?"

"Inebriated," the widow said timidly, alarmed by his look.

"We'll find that old whiskey soak," Jeff said to Warman, "an' I'll have Fatty hold his head under water till he either sobers or dies. I want her taken care of! God damn!" he said fervently, then: "Sorry, ma'am." His face was a set of fixed points as he added in a voice grim as a plague: "An' I'll see Mister Thompson in mah office within the hour, I promise yuh that."

Cy hesitated. "I don't think he'll come, Jeff. He's awful cocky. Wears two pistols. He's that sort."

"He'll be there."

Lily groaned and opened her eyes.

Jeff leaned close and asked: "You got folks, honey?"

"Nebraska," she managed in a tiny voice, then: "Farmers."

"They good people?"

"Yes, sir. They don't know about me. I wanted to go out to see the good times I'd heard about. It was so dull there."

"I'd think the dull things might look passably good right now."

"Yes . . . oh, yes."

Cy whispered in Jeff's ear: "She's got a baby, that's why she wouldn't go with Thompson."

"This sure as hell's no place for a baby." Jeff turned back to the girl. "Would they take you in, your folks?"

"I think so. But . . . my baby. I don't have a husband."

"Yes, you do. Let us worry about that." He took Warman aside. "We'll marry her tuh Fatty or someone, but don't worry, she won't even have tuh see him, whoever it is. There'll be a license tuh show. And then she'll need a death certificate for the husband an' a good story to go with it. Fortunately we're good at makin' up stories."

They moved back to the patient where Jeff knelt and fished a vial out of the inside pocket of his coat.

"Jeff, I think you answered my question," Warman said, smiling.

Jeff didn't respond. He was busy carefully measuring out a few drops of laudanum, feeding it into her swollen mouth with unexpected tenderness. Not that he used the drug himself. He was a man who liked to keep his head when all around him were losing theirs. No, he kept the drug in his desk, available against a world where the doctoring was chancy, pain common, and palliatives rare.

Later he would give the girl five hundred dollars and arrange to have Yank and Banjo take her to where she could catch a train for Nebraska. He even had The Rev write her a testimonial as her pastor. None of this ever became popular knowledge. Warman heard rumors about those details but respected Jeff's reticence. Instead, he began to broadcast Jeff's virtues far and wide.

Salt Lake Billy Thompson swaggered into Jeff's office at the appointed time because Bat Masterson had hinted to him that there might be a profitable business proposition waiting. He was pretty much what Smith had expected—tall and brawny with black hair slicked with pomade, a walrus mustache in imitation of Earp, boots with silver trim, and a loud mouth. The belief was in his eyes under thick eyebrows that

112

GET 4 FREE BOOKS!

You can have the best Westerns delivered to your door for less than what you'd pay in a bookstore or online. Sign up for one of our book clubs today, and we'll send you **4 FREE* BOOKS**, worth $23.96, just for trying it out...**with no obligation to buy, ever!**

Authors include classic writers such as
LOUIS L'AMOUR, MAX BRAND, ZANE GREY
and more; PLUS new authors such as
COTTON SMITH, TIM CHAMPLIN, JOHNNY D. BOGGS
and others.

As a book club member you also receive the following special benefits:

- **30% OFF** all orders through our website & telecenter!
- **Exclusive access** to special discounts!
- **Convenient** home delivery and 10 days to return any books you don't want to keep.

There is no minimum number of books to buy,
and you may cancel membership at any time.
See back to sign up!

*Please include $2.00 for shipping and handling.

YES!

Sign me up for the Leisure Western Book Club and send my FOUR FREE BOOKS! If I choose to stay in the club, I will pay only $13.44* each month, a savings of $10.52!

NAME: _____

ADDRESS: _____

_____

TELEPHONE: _____

E-MAIL: _____

☐ I WANT TO PAY BY CREDIT CARD.

☐ **VISA**   ☐ **MasterCard**   ☐ **DISCOVER**

ACCOUNT #: _____

EXPIRATION DATE: _____

SIGNATURE: _____

Send this card along with $2.00 shipping & handling to:

**Leisure Western Book Club
20 Academy Street
Norwalk, CT 06850-4032**

Or fax (must include credit card information!) to: 610.995.9274.
You can also sign up online at www.dorchesterpub.com.

*Plus $2.00 for shipping. Offer open to residents of the U.S. and Canada only.
Canadian residents please call 1.800.481.9191 for pricing information.

If under 18, a parent or guardian must sign. Terms, prices and conditions subject to change. Subscription subject
to acceptance. Dorchester Publishing reserves the right to reject any order or cancel any subscription.

JOIN NOW!

he was God's gift to women and feared by all men.

"I understand you're the big fish in this town, Smith," he said, pulling up a chair without being asked. Even sitting, he rested his hands close to the pistols in their silver-studded holsters, pushed out to each side. "Leastways, till Bob Ford gets his dander up."

"Oh, Bob's dander's been pretty much up for nigh on ten years, if yuh think on it," Jeff said mildly.

Thompson was looking impatient, if not bored, or more likely a little nervous. "Ain't you gonna offer me a drink?" he asked peevishly.

"Yuh know why yuh're here?"

"Well, I know who you are and you know who I am, so what's the proposition? I got just so much time to listen."

"Not quite a proposition," Jeff said, biting off the end of an expensive cigar without offering one. "What business you in, Mister Thompson?"

"Any damn' business I wanna, I 'spect. Like you." He smirked, as if they were already partnered and he was senior to Jeff.

"Runnin' a string uh girls from town to town in a wagon, the girls gettin' poked fifty times a day an' havin' no say in it. Then you take all their money an' beat 'em up good ever' once in a while just tuh show what a big fish y'all are. That the business?"

Colors ballooning one after the other, Thompson's face went from spring to deepest winter in seconds, as if he had practiced it. He began breathing like a pricked stallion.

"Or maybe just 'cause it feels good tuh beat a woman. I've know some like that. No, I think we must be in different businesses."

Thompson was on the edge of his seat now, tilting his thick torso topped by that big, swollen, red face across the desk. He had one hand on the surface and the other on a gun butt, but Soapy didn't flinch. He had his Derringer, on a watch chain, now pointed between the man's legs under the desk. Small bullets, but they didn't have to be big roaming around down there.

"What kind of pissin' in the wind is this?" Billy Thompson roared. "I come in here 'cause I thought you wanted to talk about somethin' to our mutual advantage. I don't have to take this kind a horseshit from no decked-out, desk-ridin', fancy-pants boss. You're nothin' but a swindler. To hell with you and your little shit-hole town."

Taking a calculated risk, Jeff dropped the Derringer and brought up his hands carefully to spread them on the desk top. He leaned across to meet Thompson at a point where their noses almost touched and their eyes were trying to set each other's ablaze. "I've seen the little girl we-all around here call Creede Lily," he said quietly. "Seen what yuh did tuh her."

"What's a snotty little twist like her to me? Bitch didn't appreciate what I was trying to do for her, started yellin' and screamin', so, sure, I put my hands on her. Lucky for her I didn't do more."

He put both hands on his guns now, but Jeff, as he began to rise slowly from his chair behind the desk, pulled open his coat. "I'm unarmed, Mister Thompson. I was just curious tuh see yuh for mahself 'fore ennathin' happened tuh yuh. . . ."

Thompson, rising, did jerk his guns, but he held them pointed downward at his sides. "Nothin' but big talk's gonna happen as long as I got these," he said, bringing up and brandishing the pearl-handled pistols, then spinning them.

That was not likely to impress Jeff, but Thompson lived in his own world.

"You think I can't shoot my way out of here? I'd show you if you wasn't too much of a yellow Chinaman to carry iron yourself."

Smith was easing himself around the desk with admirable calm, continuing as if he had not heard a word. "Thompson, I've gone tuh some zoos in mah time, but I haven't observed ennathin' lower down on the scale uh life's progress on this planet than what the snake leaves behind. Till now."

Thompson wasn't sure he got all of that but began to expand his heaving chest and arms on principle, cursing all the while, and made the mistake of thrusting his jaw forward and stepping in on his opponent, something that looked easy because Smith was forty pounds lighter. But Jeff was also a veteran of a hundred cow-town brawls. Thompson raised the barrel of one pistol as if to buffalo him while pointing the other in a disorderly fashion, more or less at his chest.

It was hard to know which he was going to do first, shoot or club, and he probably didn't know himself. It didn't matter. Jeff, noting the indecisiveness, moved faster than his opponent could have pulled a trigger and smashed Thompson's nose with an overhand right that knocked him back the way he had come, into the seat, stunning him. Then he called out for the boys.

Instantly Yeah Mow, who had his hatchet in his belt, Fatty, and Banjo Parker were in the room, pinning, disarming, and lifting the dazed gunman, large as he was, like a child. They looked to Soapy for guidance.

"This here's a big fella," he said. "He's rough an' wants ever'one tuh know that, too. He likes mostly tuh beat on women. I'd be curious tuh know how he fares with men, wouldn't y'all?" He stared at the terrified man, already bleeding copiously from his nose.

The three behemoths grinned in anticipation—well, two

behemoths, Fatty, of course, never smiling, although he managed to convey some eagerness to get started.

"Take him out back an' give him the works."

No one hesitated, and it was necessary for Soapy to tell the piano player in the saloon to strike up a tune in order to drown out the screams and cries for mercy. There wasn't a lot of that around, though, and, while it might not have been exactly Soapy's intention, like a lot of other intentions gone awry in the West, the pimp suffered a terrible beating.

Salt Lake's Billy Thompson's appearance afterwards was deemed sufficiently horrible to have him taken out of town in a wagon late at night without friend or fanfare. It was never determined whether or not he survived the works in some other locale.

That was the other side of the Soapy Smith gang.

It was soon made known that anyone in bad straits or harm's way could come to Jeff and have it set right. Cy Warman brought his share of broken wings and could never stop singing Smith's praises in his journal. No wronged saloon girl, widow, burned-out old sourdough, horse, or dog was ever sent away. Was it kindness or publicity, no one knew or wanted to speculate. Mattie put in her cynical two cents—those were the only kind of creatures Jeff Smith could really care about. Probably they reminded him of his mother.

One Sunday morning, as Jeff stepped out of the Tivoli, he found an itinerant preacher, Creede's first, standing out on the sunburned street, trying to sermonize to a congregation mostly indifferent and partly antagonistic. Sunday mornings always meant a lot of hangovers and bad consciences, neither of which anyone wanted to relive or recall, and it led to a certain crankiness. The preacher was probably in his thirties, wan and underfed, his hair askew. The dusty dark suit and even the Bible clutched under one arm looked well-worn. One old shoe had a hole at the tip. Still, he had a strong voice and persuasive manner. He believed, all right. He was sincere and not just some money grabber, although perhaps it hadn't been the wisest thing to choose Jeremiah as his text in this particular locale.

Jeff watched for a while, amused. It reminded him of his boyhood in Georgia. More than that, he thought the Good Book was good for people—up to a point, of course. Some of the Sunday idlers were downright rude cat-callers, but Jeff accepted that as a part of the calling. If you were going to preach at people, some were going to preach on their own right back. Still, the man's wretched appearance and youthful earnestness created some sympathy.

"Ain't no Jehovah in Creede, scarecrow," a still-drunk miner bellowed at him, "and, if he shows up, we'll run him out! Tar and feather him, that's what we'll do." Whereupon the man fell down and got several laughs, but whether for his words or the tumble it was hard to tell.

Jeff was on his way to remind the group about minding their manners on the Sabbath or else, when another, angrier example of liquored-up town trash yelled: "Take your god-damned psalm singin' out uh here, dog dirt. We don't need no Bible-thumpers. We need more girls and better liquor!" The man looked around expecting approval—"Right, boys?"—and evidently thought he had received it, because he was encouraged to pick up a piece of not entirely dry horse droppings and throw it. The preacher received it smack in the face, putting a stop to even his zealotry.

While a goodly group whooped and laughed at this comedy, the preacher recovered enough to look at his assailant and utter a soft: "I forgive you, brother."

It was a question whether Jeff heard that or not, but he had

117

his own answer to such capers and laid the long barrel of his Colt across the skull of the miscreant, dropping him like a stone in a well. The man lay there, groaning just a little bit, bleeding a lot. Jeff stood over him but ignored his plight except to move his always well-shined boots out of the way of the flowing blood.

Looking into the silent, awed faces of the idlers, Jeff told them: "Easy tuh see where a little preachin' wouldn't do enna yuh enna harm. I'll tell yuh, though, this good man here's gonna need a church tuh do it in. Give yuh a reason for that Saturday night bath. Somewhere useful to go on Sunday mornin's so yuh don't end up sinnin' like him," he said, indicating his victim. " 'Course, buildin' a proper church needs money." He pulled out a twenty. "And here's mah contribution. I expect, in light uh yuhr bad manners right out here in God's sunshine, y'all want to contribute as a . . . well . . . penance. Am I right?"

He took off his hat and passed it. No one refused to put something in. Anyone who hesitated got looked at hard and fast until he broke. It helped that Jeff kept his bloodstained pistol in his hand.

Hats were passed in all the saloons south of the line, and Creede soon had its first church, the Creede Evangelical. When Bob Ford heard about it, he tried to find out how much Soapy had contributed and, when he couldn't, gambled that it would still be outdone by a hundred. Actually, by then, it was over a thousand, and Jeff had even had an organ shipped from Denver.

The grateful preacher, who had introduced himself as Jedekiah Oliphant, felt so obliged that, when Jeff or any members of the gang were around, he tried to tailor his sermons to avoid such topics as the evils of violence, gambling, coveting, drinking, theft, avarice, deceit. . . . One result was a lot of singing, the likes of "Jesus, Lover of My Soul" and "Sweet Hour of Prayer". Then, when Mattie and some of her girls began attending, Oliphant had to drop any references pertaining to sins of the flesh to his list of excised topics. It did have the effect of creating in him a truly flexible Bible student. They never did find anyone who could play the new organ, so an accordion was substituted.

What was Bob Ford doing all this time, people wanted to know. Business was down considerably at the Exchange and his other enterprises, the street in front nearly empty after nine or ten o'clock, while the sounds of hilarity and rampant spending that drifted up on the south wind were a constant reproach and goad. Yet Ford's hired *pistoleros* seemed preoccupied with something, slouching in and out of town, acting secretively. Several new faces appeared, but no one faced up to Jeff's new supremacy as might be expected.

Rumors were the stuff of life in a place this isolated, and most of the inhabitants drooled at the prospect of further strife . . . that is, entertainment. Ford was said to be hoarding his resources and adding to them, sending out a call for the most ferocious outlaws in the West to come and join him. Smith laughed when told. Why not? The town and its people were his, while the telegraph *clicked* on and on and. . . .

Chapter Thirteen

Bob Ford's infertile but very restless mind had its big scheme and its little one, and, if the latter worked, he might not have to go to the big, expensive, risky one. The bartender, Gus, victim of Jeff's colorful entry into Creede, was reputed to be hiding up in the mountains at some friend's claim where he spent his days chewing wood and spitting out the splinters to assuage his anger. Bob sent men out to look for him.

Finally the recluse was escorted down to Creede for a meeting in Ford's office above the Exchange—in the middle of the night. There was a reason for this, and for Gus's self-imposed exile. He had refused to shave off the half of his mustache that remained. No, sir, it had been the pride of his life and no son-of-a-bitch was going to take what was left from him, not over his dead body. The problem, though, was in the way he looked with half of a handlebar. People had found it hilarious. He had been asked did the other half die and go to heaven, or was it true he had only one oyster, or had he been scalped by a drunken Indian? Naturally he had tried to discourage all this, but, as much as they might have been afraid of large, ferocious, big, mean Gus, they hadn't been able to repress their ribaldry to save their lives. Even dogs, it seemed to him, had been barking at him. It was a rock and a hard place: pride wouldn't let him get rid of the unsullied half, and pride couldn't bear the humiliation of being laughed at in the streets. It had driven him right out of town.

Ford made him a proposition at that candlelit meeting. He

had in his desk a mustache made of human hair the same color as what remained of Gus's and the glue to apply it. Ford announced that he had sent all the way to Denver for it. It only needed to be cut in half, and the other half would give Gus a spare. He would get it and five hundred dollars for a certain little errand.

Soon word was all over Creede, as it was intended to be, that Gus was back and determined to get revenge for his lost honor. The story, as it went from drinker to drinker and bar to bar, was of a challenge. Sure, Soapy had a lot of tough men working for him, but if he wasn't a low coward, he would come out in the daylight and face Gus alone in the street.

Mattie related the rumors to Jeff one night as he sat, watching her prepare herself for the evening, brushing her hair, applying make-up. He had a glass of wine and a cigar and was sitting sideways behind her, thinking this was one of life's finer occasions, watching a woman do herself up for men. He could have watched all night.

As for the rumor, he had heard it several times in one form or another. "But I have yet to see the gentleman doin' all this talkin'."

"You wouldn't do it, would you? Let him call you out?"

"I don't wallow 'round in the streets with trash, Mattie. You ought tuh know that."

"Yeah, but I know men, too. If you so much as hint their pecker wouldn't win a race with a pickle, they want to kill the whole world and don't care a hoot if they live or die."

Jeff chuckled and tried to reassure her.

"Don't laugh, I know this big ox better than you."

"Not in the usual way, I hope."

She emitted a professional, long-practiced sigh. "Jeff, has it escaped your notice that now, and for some time now, I have been . . . Mattie Silks has been . . . an entrepreneur. I have been ever since I came to this god-forsaken place. Maybe you can see where I was a little grateful to a couple of pond dwellers like Bob and Claude for setting me up here."

"You're top of the pile, all right, I see that. But there's still such a thing as the boss samplin' the merchandise, putting his, or her, hand in."

It was mostly banter on his part, but love was a subject Mattie generally took seriously.

"Oh, God, men are dumb. If I ever spent anywhere near the time on my back you think, I'd have bedsores for life. The sex part's the small part of what we do. I can't tell you how many times some lonely fella's cried all over us when they can't raise the flag 'cause they miss the missus or their pals or some little back-house town, and they can't go back 'cause they told everybody they'd make a pile and all they got is holes in their socks. We end up mending them a lot. That's what it's really like. The other part . . . it's over so quick, half the time we don't know we're even doin' it."

Jeff was experiencing a rare embarrassment. "Hell, Mattie, I know all that. How long you think I been in the game?" He decided to be honest. "I'm still jealous."

"Well, you don't have to be, sugar. I'm yours now and only yours. And I don't notice you turning a cold hand to the skills I've learned in the trade."

"I'd be a fool."

She had been watching him in the mirror but now she turned around and looked at him, wearing only her corset and crossing her marvelous legs. "Jeff, have you got any idea what love is?"

"Some," he acknowledged grudgingly. "I figure it's about the most lied-about subject in the world."

That made Mattie a little grim. "Maybe so, but for a lot of us it still has some luster."

"Why don't yuh hurry up there, honey. I'm gettin' hungry."

"And you haven't heard a word I've said, have you?"

Maybe not, but watching her in the mirror had given him an idea.

"All this bushwa about meeting you in the street . . . ?" she continued. "He'll shoot you in the back when you step out of the Tivoli one night. Or, if he says it's six-guns in the sunlight, you know he'll bring a shotgun somehow or have a snake in a window somewheres. You'll have to watch every window or doorway for blocks. And it's all a scheme, Jeff, you know that. Bob Ford's behind it."

"I know it."

"That all you're gonna say?"

"Mattie, I've been around a while but I'm no duelist. Can't hit ennathin' with a rifle, so all mah work 'long that line's been from ten feet away in a saloon, where I must've been reasonably successful as I'm still standin' here, don't yuh know. But, on the other hand, I don't show mah back tuh enna one."

"God help you."

"I'll help mahself an' He can watch."

Mattie crossed herself.

The excitement built in such a way that any fool would know it was orchestrated. Jeff said it was Bob's theatrical background that made him good at it, and he had no intention of falling into his trap. Not everyone was as sympathetic, however, as the gang. Part of the talk inevitably was to the effect that Mr. King of the Hill, Soapy Smith, was dodging his challenger, afraid to meet him man to man, or even answer to the complaint. Hadn't he given Gus all the justification in the world, humiliating him like that, ripping the manhood right

123

off the man's face? Even a bartender has his pride.

Jeff loved faro and insisted on playing it in someone else's casino where the game wouldn't be fixed in his favor. He had to have that factor of risk in order to enjoy it. Indulging that little eccentricity had cost him fortunes. Stepping out of one of those saloons at two in the morning after having blown a whole week's take from his three establishments and all the rackets south of the line, he was, uncharacteristically, a little drunk. Few people hated to lose at anything as much as Jeff Smith. It was his weakness and he hated it, but then everyone in his line seemed to have one.

Proceeding not too steadily up the rutted main street, he was counting the few serendipitous dollars he had just discovered in his vest pocket. When the shotgun went off behind him, he failed to react with the usual dash, standing there for a moment, wondering if he had been hit before throwing himself into the dust of the street.

It was the sound of running feet that sobered and energized him. The shot had come from twenty-five or thirty yards behind him. There was still smoke hanging in the still summer air at the entrance to a little passageway between the feed store and assay office. He jumped to his feet, jerked his pistol on the run, and in seconds banished that smoke plume by ripping through it.

As he came out into the open field behind the stores, someone fired a pistol at him, two shots, and once again he was forced to hug the earth, burying his face because the shots sounded very close. He raised his head carefully, looked around—buildings, rocks, trees, the chaotic mixture of the natural and the ramshackle that was Creede—but he couldn't see or hear anything. Perhaps if he had reacted sooner.

It wasn't until he was once more on his feet that he understood he had been hit. Nothing major, two pellets through his coat and shirt into the arm, another in the back that had barely penetrated the flesh. A little bleeding, that was all. He felt badly about the coat. Mattie or one of the boys would take the pellets out and clean the wounds. He couldn't be absolutely certain who it was, but he knew this: it was a coward. Sure, anyone who bushwhacked a man in a city street from behind with a shotgun was by definition a coward, but in this case the shooter went beyond that. He had been so afraid of Jeff that he had hesitated to fire until his victim was well past, and even then his aim was on the shaky side. Had he had the oysters to fire at Soapy when he was abreast of him, it would have been " 'crost the plain" for Mrs. Smith's Saturday night communicant. At least, Jeff thought, he had learned not to take Mattie's wisdom lightly.

That the great Soapy Smith had been shot, ambushed, bushwhacked, was all over Creede by morning. Maybe one of Mattie's girls had betrayed it. Certainly none of the gang would have. Most likely the shooter had guessed he had hit Smith, and Bob Ford had seen an opportunity. Even if it wasn't true, it would suit Ford's purposes.

The stakes rose and excitement built. One rumor had it that Jeff had run away as if the devil pursued him. Most people, and everyone who knew Jeff personally, rejected that out of hand, but there was considerable sentiment to suggest he would have to answer the provocation now or be branded a coward himself. The betting grew heavy.

Cy Warman, having no choice, reported the situation in the *Candle* that afternoon. A feud of such proportions was the woof and warp of Creede and any journalist who didn't cover it would have been run out of town. Naturally he slanted it to what he saw as being in Jeff's favor, arguing that the man who had brought unparalleled law and order to the once-violent streets of the town was not obligated to go out into the dust of one of them and tangle with bullies and back-shooters. **Put up to it by we all know who, don't we?**

Jeff actually wanted it over by any means whatsoever, but, for reasons of legality, not to speak of his standing in the community, he kept that and his intentions to himself. He arrived at the Tivoli for lunch, as was his habit, to find the place crowded and buzzing. With his nonchalant persona it was easy to pretend that he didn't notice, when he would have to be deaf and blind not to.

Syd came to join him at the bar, where everyone else was hanging back, to report on matters. Jeff listened, nodding. First reported was the routine business of the night before, who had to be paid what, anything new in town or in from Denver, and finally what the crowd was watching and waiting for, the excitement of the day.

"Yuh think," Jeff observed wryly, and indicated the gapers who were pretending not to gape, "yuh could get them all tuh do a little drinkin' an' gamblin' . . . we don't make enna money off gawkin'."

Soon certain members of the drinking fraternity were sidling up, full of concern and friendly intentions to report things. Gus had been seen standing drinks in the palace this morning, bragging about how he was going to settle Soapy Smith once and for all. And, boy, was he ever surrounded by a bunch of hard-looking, well-armed sympathizers.

An old miner came in and said that now Gus had moved on to the Bonanza where he was "workin' hisself up pretty good, sayin' things like . . . 'I'm gonna part Soapy Smith's hair down to his neck and he won't need no hat no more.' Them's his exact words. And he was wearin' two pistols."

"Yuh see enna sign of a shotgun?"

"No, sir, I didn't."

"Must have it in his drawers, is all I can think."

Jeff thanked him for the intelligence and ordered a steak sandwich from the kitchen and a bottle of beer from the bartender.

As he ate, he listened to another first-hand report that Gus had moved to the El Dorado and was standing drinks all around, saying: "Soapy Smith don't have no idea what he's up 'g'inst. They can start work on boot hill right now, 'cause I will have my revenge today."

A few minutes later Bat came in and volunteered to arrest Gus, and anyone with him, for disturbing the peace. "Keep him in the calaboose till he either grows back his mustache or dies from the shame of it."

Jeff chuckled. "Won't never grow back, I'm afraid. I took it out by the roots." He clapped Masterson on the shoulder and thanked him. "No need for yuh tuh get inta it, Bat. It's mah play, mah call. He keeps goin' from one saloon to 'nother, he'll be too soused tuh do ennathin' ennaway."

He invited Bat to join him for lunch, but the sheriff said he had to be out and around on a day like this, keep his eyes and ears open.

The reports kept coming in. It was obviously going to be a long, tedious day unless Gus made a move soon. One man quoted the lethal bartender as saying that, if Soapy didn't come out before sundown and meet him face to face, he was a "yella skunk".

Assuming that everyone who could was listening anyway, Jeff looked around and announced: "Now that'd be a sight tuh see . . . a yella skunk. Y'all ever seen one uh them? Makes yuh kind uh wonder, don't it, which part's yella, the stripe or the skunk around it?"

The tension was such that he got a huge laugh from the assemblage.

Then Mattie marched in for what she claimed was a glass

of champagne, but admitted that she was getting damned tired of pacing around the Library and had to see her lover in the flesh to know he was all right.

"Why wouldn't I be?"

"Jeff, where's the gang?" she asked, looking around, alarmed.

"I told 'em tuh stay away. They're prob'ly lurkin' somewheres, but I don't want 'em in here. Like I needed 'em an' can't watch out for mahself."

"Oh, sweet Jesus."

He looked at her and shook his head, amused at her unexpected tenderness. "What is this, Mattie, a last visit tuh the condemned man? Don't look so blue, honey."

She was too worried to scold or nag and put her head down on his shoulder, saying: "Oh, sweetheart, I'm scared."

He moved her away brusquely, whispering: "What's wrong with yuh? There's people lookin' here. I can't have 'em seein' that."

Mattie was in so much distress that she accepted even this small rudeness, or understood the need for it. Still, it was more fortunate than she would ever know that she had come, for she was in a position to do him a great service by way of telling him the tale of how Ford had procured Gus's fake mustache. Mattie, in her antebellum gloom, didn't even think it was funny, but Jeff laughed so hard he discombobulated everybody, including her. There were a few whispers that the strain had driven him mad. His friends didn't think that, but they were concerned. He felt so good afterwards that he sent Mattie on her way with a big public hug and kiss that got everybody in the saloon back on a comparatively even keel.

Last to come in, about four o'clock, to show their concern

were what Jeff had taken to calling privately the "un-holy three"—Holy, Cameron, and Schumhaldter—plus Cy Warman, after putting his story to bed. They found Jeff reading week-old New York papers and one from Denver published just the day before. Had he read today's story in the *Candle*? Jeff said about twenty times, a word at a time, whenever someone thrust it in front of him.

"Man can't drink in peace in his own saloon enna more."

Collectively the three urged him to accept Cy's advice: to refuse to take the bait, refuse to go out. A public duel in the street would not only be dangerous for him, but bad for the town. Besides, it was against the law.

Jeff turned to Cy and asked, since he had written the piece, if that was what he believed? Cy said he had done what he thought was consistent with his rôle as a responsible journalist, but he didn't think it right to give individuals advice on how to conduct their lives when that advice might be harmful to them, and he suspected that Jeff was a man who had his own compass, anyway, and would answer to it. Smith liked that. He just stood there and smiled. He knew the temper and temperature of a town like this, knew that, if he didn't face down this fool who wanted to kill him for no good reason and with the help of God knows how many accomplices, he would be branded a coward.

Maybe the question on the table was who would really run Creede? He tried to make it sound like a joke when he said: "You boys suggestin' that it's illegal puts me in kind of a bind here, don't yuh think? If I go out, I'm a criminal an' a hypocrite, an' if I don't, I'm a yella hypocrite."

They assured him that this was not their intention and would back him no matter what happened. People would have to understand.

Jeff glanced at his pocket watch. He was beginning to feel

edgy. *What the hell was taking so long?* He knew there was all that drinking and bragging to be done, but the day was passing and with it the bright light he wanted outside.

The doors swung open as they had all day, but Smith knew somehow that this wasn't it. Pony Bill had come to act as second for the offended, although he was ready to admit that he wasn't exactly sure what that meant. He appeared nervous and a little awed by the saloon, one in which he had never set foot, hostile ground, its clientele as jittery and excited as a colony of ants.

"You Soapy Smith?" Pony Bill asked.

Jeff unashamedly ratcheted his voice up to public speaking. They wanted a show, well, he would give them one, go right out on stage for the rest of the drama. "Yuh just know I am. Step on over tuh the bar, son, an' have a drink. We won't bite yuh."

Forehead scrunched in the struggle to remember what he had been told to say, Bill shook it off. "I'm here to deliver an important message, if I can git it all. . . ."

"Say, don't y'all work for Bob Ford?"

Stymied, Bill hesitated a moment, and then said: "Naw. He told me to tell you I don't. I'm just . . . a good friend of Gus . . . uh, the bartender, you know. He told me. . . ."

By now a lot of the crowd in the saloon was trying unsuccessfully to restrain laughter. Bill looked around, angry and bewildered.

"Never mind them," Jeff said, reaching out to turn Bill's attention back to the matter at hand. "I sure as hell seen you somewheres." He remembered very well where he had first seen Gus's "second" and where he had seen him since, but sowing confusion in the ranks of his enemies was one of Soapy's basic strategies. "Yuh know this one?" He hummed "Rose of Tralee" and had the gratification of seeing the cowboy's eyes expand with alarm.

"Where'd you hear that?"

"How 'bout yuh give me Gus the bartender's message an' y'all can go on out uh here an' do whatever it is yuh do for Bob."

Sweat had leaped upon Pony Bill's forehead and was dancing a jig on it. "Could I have that whiskey now . . . clean?"

Jeff signaled the bartender who served up a shot. Jeff watched the cowboy gulp it, wanting to get this whole business over with.

Bill wiped his lips and tried to look bold. "You are to know that my frien' Gus is waitin' in the street out there for you right now. And he says if you don't come out to face him man to man, he will have to find other ways to avenge his honor."

"I believe we already saw that at work last night," Jeff observed wryly. "Go on."

"An' . . . an' also . . . no man could blame him. An' . . . could I have another of them whiskies?" Jeff nodded, looking at his audience and shaking his head. "An' he said, furthermore, if you don't come out now, you are a yeller skunk. That's all he said." He looked around at the crowd anxiously. "It wasn't me said that. The last part."

"So, y'all want me tuh go out inta that hot, dirty street right now an' shoot it out with a bartender, that it? Who's he think he is, Wyatt Earp? Wild Bill? Some kind uh clown in the circus, is all I see. First, I don't fight with creatures so low-down in the history uh human development as this ape."

"Huh?" said Pony Bill. "Wha. . . . ?"

"Yuh tell yuhr new pard this . . . can yuh remember?"

Bill nodded with a vigor he didn't feel, he just wanted out of this crazy house.

"Never yuh mind, boy. Tell him this . . . I'm afraid to go

out there . . ."—he took a stage wait while his audience gasped, whether amazed or horrified, it didn't matter which—"afraid that, if I see that face toupee he's got on his lip, I might die uh laughter." He gave the audience a moment to recover their faith. The tormented look on Bill's face caused him to explain: "That's French for a piece uh fake hair yuh're s'posed tuh put on yuhr head, but I guess ol' Gus couldn't find his own scalp. Don't know why, the way it shines in the light. By the by, is it true what I hear . . . that hair comes from nuns?"

All Bill could think to say was: "I think it looks real good. Cost Bob a lot of money."

"But what if we're standin' out there with our faces all grim, our hands on the butts of our pistols, ready for one uh us tuh die, an' then the damn' wind blows it off? There I am, fallin' down an' wallowin' 'round in the dirt an' horseshit, holdin' mah sides and we ain't even pulled yet? I'd be helpless. Or a dog mistakes it for a wiener an' bites it off? What about that? Or some kid or a monkey could come along an' mistake it for the hangin' branches of a willa tree an' start swingin' on it, an' there I am helpless from merriment ag'in. Yuh see the problem I got here? Where's the fair fight in that?"

Bill, the one man left out of the joke, had finally turned surly. "I don't know all you're sayin', but you're sure havin' fun with me, ain't you? Well, Gus ain't gonna find it so funny an' he ain't gonna like it no ways, neither." Frowning, he added: "If I can remember half of it."

That brought more laughter.

"This mean you ain't gonna fight him?" the cowboy persisted, dogged if nothing else.

"Yuh tell him what I said and what all these good people here heard me say, much as yuh got hold uh. If it don't sit well with him, he knows where I'll be. Now git."

Pony Bill wasn't sure how he could make a prideful exit after these bastards had made such a spectacle of him. So he had to think about it for a moment before he spat on the floor, turned, and stalked out with his hand on his pistol, staring straight ahead—to continuing laughter from the bravery of crowds.

Jeff could actually see how his neck turned red. He had to hope that this dim cowboy would carry the message of his humiliation all the way to Gus—everything depended upon it.

Chapter Fourteen

Waiting, Jeff positioned himself in front of a corner of the large mirror behind the bar. He stood with his back to the front entrance but had a perfect view, nonetheless. A quiet word to the bartenders made certain that they wouldn't obscure his view for even a few seconds. It was something that Bob Ford was said to have used in the past to his advantage.

As unobtrusively as possible he requested that the windows be closed, saying that the slanting rays of the setting sun were bringing heat into the room. It was considerably darkened, but no one seemed to mind. They went back to their games and drinking, the ones bold enough to stay around, with one eye and one ear tuned to the situation.

Jeff invited Holy's bunch to join him at the bar and discuss plans he had for forming a Creede baseball team. He had done some preliminary figures and even some drawings. He was prepared to provide the land and equipment so long as he could be the pitcher.

Cy Warman said he had to get back to the paper, but Smith told him to stick around, since he was pretty sure that before long there would be a story big enough for an extra edition. Cy took the hint, although it made him a little nervous, and he kept glancing over his shoulder at the swinging doors.

Jeff murmured: "I'd be obliged if yuh didn't do that, Cy." He disguised his reason with smiling self-depreciation: "Yuh're gettin' me a little nervy." He wanted anyone coming through that door with a pointed gun to confront a target that seemed totally unaware.

Cy could hear the damned big clock behind the bar ticking and ticking and wished he didn't until it became something like the Chinese water torture for him. *Tick . . . tick. . . .* Even the usual *clink* of glasses was muted.

It had become so mournfully quiet that Soapy would have been glad of an argument or a fight. Finally he asked someone to go and roust the piano player from bed, or wherever he was, and put him to work.

He had counted on an immediate reaction to his provocation, now that the sun was going down and he would lose the advantage inherent in someone's coming out of the bright light into the dark. But just when he was beginning to despair of everything he had so carefully laid out, the swinging doors, untouched for half an hour, were kicked open. A lot of people started, but only a few dared to sneak a look.

Silhouetted by the bright light outside, blinking as his pupils raced to expand, stood the outsize figure, a portrait, really, of the man who had hated Soapy Smith since the day of his arrival in Creede. There was no mistaking him. Besides his rejuvenated huge mustache, he held in his hands a large, double-barreled shotgun and on his face a look that would terrify the meek. What was also there was puzzlement. Where was his target among all those barely discernible black suits lined up along the bar, frozen in place like a daguerreotype?

Jeff watched him in the mirror just long enough to steady himself, but he had to hope not long enough for Gus to do the same. His hand, staying close to the body, slid snake-like down to the butt of the Colt and pulled it with the same smooth motion. In the mirror, the shotgun was already up and turning in his general direction. How huge it looked with its twin, gaping volcano mouths eager to mangle him and shred the remains before they reached the floor.

He could sense the men around him, could feel, hear, smell their fear as they spun, saw, fled, or ducked away from the horror to come, leaving him to stand alone. But if it was carnage they anticipated, there was none.

"Soapy Smith?" Gus bellowed, without directing it anywhere specific. Then, chillingly: "There you are, you son-of-a. . . ."

Jeff, too, had instinctively spun around, screwing himself down into a crouch while putting the gun out in front, actually sighting and firing one, two, three shots a half second apart, then one more, saving one against the vicissitudes of poor aim. He had heard of people firing from the hip, but it didn't make sense to him.

Two of the first three struck Gus in the chest and stomach. The shotgun jumped high with the shock, and one barrel went off, bringing down a rain of plaster and shards from a chandelier. The last one hit him in the thigh, but he was already tumbling to the ground. His knees buckled so that he bent backwards in a grotesque attitude. He screamed, as much in fury as anguish, with some of the air whistling obscenely out of a hole in his lung. The shotgun was thrown as much as dropped and *clanged* along the floor.

Jeff didn't move for a moment. No one did. The atmosphere was heavy with blue smoke and an acrid odor, but there were no other sounds than those from Gus, not even of heavy breathing, as people had suspended even their heartbeats. Then, of course, pandemonium: a few night birds wailed, men bellowed, people ran in all directions as if surprised and alarmed by the very show they had waited hours to see. A table was tipped over in the rush, throwing chips, bets, and cards to the floor amid cries of rage. Some glasses crashed to the floor while others rushed to the bar to get their glasses filled.

At first no one came close to shooter or shot, leaving them in well-defined little pools of isolation from humankind, two souls too close to death to be borne for the moment. Holy Moses and Cy Warman did inquire if Jeff was all right.

Tight-faced, he allowed as how he was. People here knew enough to respect that. He would remain so even when the prevailing madness had passed and people were clapping him on the back and pelting him with congratulations, just as they would have done with Gus had he won, and Jeff knew that, too. Anyway, his job at the moment was to disguise the inner tremor.

They buried Gus with a full mustache and everyone applauded the sentiment. Soapy paid for the funeral as Bob Ford did not like being associated with a loser, especially this one.

"Spread out, boys," Kelly ordered his band. "And look good, 'cause I'm gettin' damned sick of all this. God have mercy, it shouldn't be this hard to find."

"What's it look like?" Cale asked.

They were still coming down off of a rocky hillside toward the stream.

"Like your neck, long and skinny. What the hell you think a cable looks like? A donkey's ass has got more brains than you."

There were twelve now in Bob's employ and more arriving every day. This bunch, looking for the source of the telegraph, numbered five. Ford, unwilling to show his hand until he had overwhelming odds in his favor, didn't want his men, especially the newcomers, wandering around town, stirring talk, so he had sent most of them to an encampment in the hills.

Right now the five were several miles from town, searching

lower Willow Creek for Soapy's telegraph source, whatever that turned out to be, in the hope that they could stop it there or, if not, rip it out by the roots somewhere along the way. That would be the end of Soapy's popularity, or so Bob Ford thought.

Some rode their ponies right into the chilly water, where it was shallow, moving in circles up and down its length. Others waded around near the banks, trying to feel beneath the tumbling surface with their hands or a long knife. It would not have been difficult to follow the cable from right where it left town, but they had once more been ordered to be discreet and seek it at some distance where no one would see them. The problem was the streams and creeks kept branching off in all directions through all sorts of terrain. They ran shallow and then deep, forcing the posse to ride up a mountain to find the source and back down to where it simply disappeared into a bog or a hole only to reappear somewhere else.

Some of the boys were beginning to suspect they were the victims of just the sort of shenanigans for which Soapy Smith's gang was famous—always having their joke and making others look like fools. All they knew for certain was that they were cold, tired, and bored, longing for the warm comfort of the saloons and saloon girls. They had brought whiskey with them, and a couple of the men had been drunk since they started, which did nothing for their efficiency. One, reputed to have killed ten men, kept falling off his mount and needed help every time to get back on.

Now, at last, they were convinced that they had found the right stream, were on the right scent. There was a wild shout from Cale—"I got it, I got it!"—and then a scream loud enough to make the mountains quiver.

"What's that? What happened?" Kelly yelled from downstream, and came riding full bore, getting very wet.

A disgusted Lev told him it was a snake.

They did discover it finally, as they were bound to, not the source, but the cable itself. With obvious joy they set to work vigorously destroying it in every way that brought pleasure—wire cutters, buck knives, dragging it from the saddle, throwing dynamite into the water, even trying to shoot it.

Lev said: "Jist like cuttin' old Soapy Smith's joog-ler vein."

The explosions particularly excited the group. Cale cried: "Better'n the circus!"

"Well, boys," Kelly said, "we finally got somethin' to tell ol' Bob that'll please him." They whirled their mounts back toward town full tilt, whooping and hurrahing their success.

Chapter Fifteen

"There you go," Yank said as the *clacking* stopped, "that's seven and a half dollars' worth of message."

The old prospector, standing next to him on the porch of the Library, squinted and read Yank's scrawl slowly: " 'Remember the things we held so dear. Return to your hearthside and have no fear.' " He shook his head. "That don't sound like Maude, but then I left her over twenty year ago." He counted out the money in coins.

Yank reassured him: "Sometimes I put in a little poetry. That's my real vocation."

"Oh, that's all right, that's all right. I like a bit a poetry."

The old man wandered off. Yank called for the next customer to step up, happily raking it in and oblivious of the distant sound of galloping hoof beats. People on the street, however, were beginning to turn an anxious ear.

Kelly's raiding party was preceded by the huffing and clopping of horses, then the men, who were weary, mud-splattered, ominous in the way they regarded the ordinary citizens who dared give them a glance, yet exultant. They had come to the Library to gloat, with Kelly's smirk leading them right up to the porch. Yank gave them a nervous look. The customer of the moment said he would come back later, and quiet immediately drenched the scene. Only the horses violated it with their chronic restiveness.

Enjoying their triumph, the boys all laughed, circling their horses, preening, drinking in the saddle. One threw his empty bottle into the air, and a couple shot at it and missed. They shouted for the girls to come out and the citizens to get off the street, as if they needed to be told. By God, the joke was theirs now and they would let the rest of the town in on the truth when they were good and ready.

Suddenly the telegraph receiver began *clacking,* sounding downright raucous in that tense atmosphere, and causing Yank to jump. The cowboys were stunned.

"It's still alive!" Lev shouted, yanking on the reins so abruptly that it caused his horse to rear and lunge all over the street. No one laughed now.

Someone shouted: "It can't be. We killed it!"

Cale gave a strangled cry and, when he had regained control of his own horse, rode it right up onto the porch after Yank.

One thing Fewclothes was good at was escape. Instantly he grabbed up his instrument and rushed inside, slamming and locking the door behind him. His pursuer rode up to it, hung low in the saddle, and pounded on the stout wood with his gun butt, screaming curses and demanding to be let in.

Windows began popping open above as the soiled doves reacted to all this racket in the morning, not their best time. One, Big Bertha, with curlers in her hair, cream on her face, a tone like a hundred crows, and a voice like a Flügelhorn, yelled down: "What the hell you want this hour, horse boy?"

Cale directed his mount back far enough to where he could look up past the porch roof. "Let us in there, Bertha, god-dammit!"

A Chinese girl, Happy Wu or Wu Happy, no one ever got it straight, yelled: "We no work now! Come back later. But take bath first, OK?"

Several girls howled, as only whores can.

Bertha added: "And leave your horse outside, honey. We don't got anyone here can accommodate him."

By now, even the timid had crept back onto the street in order to share in the entertainment. Kelly, furious but too confused to act upon it, ordered his men to give it up for now and herded them off in the direction of the Exchange.

With Yank, Mattie came out onto the porch to watch them go. "Whatever do you s'pose got them so upset?"

The telegraph *clacked* a caustic counterpoint to the fading hoof beats.

"I'm tellin' you, we cut it and cut it good and we shot it and throwed dynamite on it and rode the horses over it, and it's still workin'."

Ford shouted something about them not knowing a snake from a telegraph wire.

Lev started—"As a matter of fact, Bob. . . ."—but the rest was lost. Some said they had never heard Bob Ford so out of sorts.

When the gang had left, actually having been thrown out, Ford paced for a while and eventually paused before one of those highly romanticized wall posters from his theatrical days showing him conquering all with two blazing guns. It was enough to make a not very contemplative man contemplate where the hell he had gone wrong. He thought that now he knew—restraint.

There was the usual carrying on at the Tivoli that night. Yank had written a song about Soapy and was accompanied by Banjo.

These words we hear as he hollers his wares,
To the unwashed hordes on our thoroughfares. . . .

142

Bowers brought some papers over to the bar where Jeff was standing with Syd. Placing them in front of Jeff and pointing out certain figures, he said: "Made eleven thousand yesterday and last night, even allowing for that new dealer with the sticky hands."

"Run him off or let Fatty have a talk with him, whichever's most humane." Jeff pushed the figures over in front of Syd.

"Ford's Exchange's practically deserted. That whole end of town is," Bowers said.

The news didn't make Gentleman Syd happy. "You get a loony like Ford completely in the shit hole, that's when you better watch out."

"Now, Syd might just be right there, Soapy. Maybe we oughta hire us some *pistoleros,* too. Most of us aren't fightin' men, come right down to it."

Jeff thought it over and shook his head. "We're the law an' order boys, remember. Moses and the city council wouldn't like it one bit. Right now, Ford's their problem. Let's keep it that way." He looked into two long faces.

"Only reason they're not afraid of him," Syd pointed out, "was we weren't."

Jeff gripped them both by a shoulder. "Now yuh boys just stand there an' fret all night. But I got some fancy courtin' tuh do."

"Jeff," Bowers inquired, "haven't you already had carnal knowledge of that young lady about a hundred times?"

"Just shows yuh how late I am with the courtin'."

He went off whistling, leaving the two at the bar.

Syd ordered another whiskey. "Jeff's brilliant at figuring, but poor on worrying."

Mattie came out of her room at the Library, still applying make-up on the move, only to catch two of her girls trying to peek through the keyhole of the forbidden room.

"You two get away from there, you hear me! Can't you read?"

The girls were embarrassed and a little frightened. The first said: "We was jist a little curious."

"What killed the cat," Mattie reminded her, pointing. "You think that sign's humorous?"

The other girl was more defiant. "The big hippo went out and there's nobody inside so we didn't see no harm. . . ."

Mattie slapped her face. "You hear me? I ever catch you two peekin' in there again and you'll be backwards on a mule to Denver with you painted black. That clear enough?"

Pouting, they flounced down the stairs ahead of her.

It was a warm summer night, but not so far into summer that the birds and crickets had given up advertising for a mate or the last spring blossoms had fallen from the trees and flowers. There was a cool breeze as was customary at that elevation after a certain hour, so Mattie had worn her serape, a very high-toned one she claimed had been made for the Empress Carlotta of Mexico. Considering what a good bad shot she had turned out to be, no one questioned it.

Jeff had rented a buggy because, as he explained with telling logic, he could hardly take her out to one of the saloons or cafés where they spent every night anyway. Mattie liked it out here under the lee of the High Sierras, immaculate stars flung across the blue-black sky everywhere you looked. There were night sounds and the creaking of the wheels, the huffing of the horse. Jeff's arm was around her, even if his pistol was giving her a bruise.

"Not often a gentleman wants to entertain me out of doors. And call it 'courtin', at that."

Jeff pulled the buggy to a halt under some trees and pro-

144

duced an ornate flask. "It's French, honey. Eighteen Thirty-Three."

She held her cigar out to the side so she could take in the odor, sighing and asking—"You trying to seduce me, Jeff Smith, with all these fancy ways?"—while he poured the brandy into two silver cups. "You truly are a gentleman."

"In mah fashion, Mattie, in mah fashion."

Her spirits seemed to subside for a moment, staring out into the darkness for something that really had to come from inside. "And I am going to be a fine lady one of these days."

"Yuh might have tuh change yuh brand uh cigars."

"Change quite a few things, sweetheart. But I could. I've got the looks and the brains and I'm learning French." She snuggled up to him.

Jeff, in a complaisant mood himself, accepted it. "What else does a woman need?"

"A man. The right man."

"I thought maybe yuh had one."

"To marry?"

"Be a lucky man tuh marry yuh, Mattie. I mean that."

"You do?"

"I'm a helluva liar, one uh the best in the country, but I wouldn't lie 'bout that."

"What about you?"

Jeff was beginning to feel it was a warmer night than he had realized and shifted uneasily in the buggy seat.

"What about me?"

She pulled free of his grasp in order to half turn and look him in the eye. "If I'd make such a damn' fine wife, why don't you marry me?"

"Me? Yuh talkin' 'bout givin' up the sportin' life?"

"You bet I am. In a couple years I'll be thirty years old."

Jeff, for the first time, looked and sounded serious. "I'm

the wrong one, Mattie." He heard hoof beats and looked be-hind.

"I know. But I can't help it."

Mattie started to kiss him, but the sound of a horse at full gallop distracted her. Jeff drew the Colt and held it across his lap while a young boy, an orphaned kid who did odd jobs around the saloons, came panting into the clearing and fought to restrain his horse, calling out: "Mister Smith . . . Mister Smith!"

"Sweet Jesus, son, what is it? Almost give me a seizure."

Mattie, frustrated just when she thought she might have been delivering the *coup de main,* was angry. "What the hell's this about now?"

"Mister Smith," the kid repeated, trying to get his breath. "Mister Dixon and The Reverend sent me. They're all gonna lynch some feller works for you, I think. You got to come quick."

"Who's lynchin' who, boy? Settle down, now." He looked at Mattie, exasperated. "I can't leave town five minutes on a personal errand but all hell breaks. Spit it out, son."

Mattie started to raise Cain about his referring to their courtship as an "errand", but the situation rode roughshod over it—men always had to have these damned men things on their pea brains.

"Uh, Mister Harris. . . ."

"Frisco Red? Frisco Red Harris?"

"Yes, sir. He shot some tinhorn, they say, gamblin' . . . an' now they're settin' to lynch him."

"Who?"

"Ever'body, I 'spect, but Mister Dixon said it was Mister Ford's bunch heavy in the crowd."

"Get off that horse. You drive the lady back." Jeff was al-ready out of the buggy. "How much time?"

146

"I don't know, but they're singin' 'bout Jeff Davis and sour apple trees. Mister Masterson, he's took a prisoner down to Santa Fé."

Jeff slipped his Colt into Mattie's hands. "Yuh never know, maybe this kid's some play uh Bob Ford's."

"Jeff, no . . . ! You'll need this."

Jeff just grinned and tapped his head. "I'll need this."

With Mattie cursing him and the kid, and Jeff cursing mankind and the horse, he tore off across country in the direction of Creede.

Chapter Sixteen

"Where in hell is ever'body?" Jeff demanded, striding the main street toward the action where, fortuitously, the mob was about to utilize the big aspen in front of the Library that had done service before as Creede's unofficial hanging tree. Bowers and Syd, the latter with a Winchester but somewhat slowed by time on the pipe, attempted to keep up.

Bowers was capable of picking up a club or a sap if he had to, but mostly he went unarmed, arguing that anything else would not be compatible with the propriety demanded of a man of the cloth. He filled Jeff in. "Moses s'posed to have gone up to protect his mine."

"I 'spect they're all off somewheres," Jeff said, "protecting something, waiting for us to settle it one way or the other."

"I tried preaching, even speaking in tongues, but there aren't a whole lot of Christians in that bunch."

Under the fatal tree they already had Red Harris, a once fierce-looking man of large size with a face like broken stone, now considerably subdued. He wore city clothes, sat astride a mule with the hemp around his neck. Some of the marks of battering appeared to be recent and his derby had been jammed back on his head in mockery. He looked over at Jeff vacantly without a lot of hope or anything else.

"Hold on now, boys, hold on!" Jeff called out, striding through the crowd to climb onto the porch of the Library across the street. The girls and their clients of the moment were hanging out of every window and doorway.

"None of your beeswax, Smith!" a voice cried from the crowd.

"We'll string you up, too, sharper!" came from another one brave in his anonymity.

Someone else joined in—"This crook shot Dick Purdy dead six times!"—initiating an argument when someone else said it wasn't Purdy but an English gambler who was only shot three times while a third claimed it was a newly arrived miner with six kids. They were all anonymous or they wouldn't have been there.

Jeff waved them down like a politician receiving a prolonged ovation. "I know, I know, I heard all 'bout it. But we got law an' order now in this town. You want tuh give that up?"

"Whose law and order, Soapy Smith? Yours?"

Jeff looked out across the throng and saw that it was Lev who had called out. He looked a bit to the left and saw Kelly grinning. A little farther on were Cal, Pony Bill, and a newcomer, Bitter Creek Johnson, and some he didn't know but had that scowling look.

"What's the matter?" Pony Bill called. "You too good for a little lynchin'?"

"Naw," Jeff said, "I can see the entertainment in it, but once yuh start this sort uh thing, yuh just never know who might be next." Such subtlety was lost on the gang, who started yelling for the crowd to get on with it. Jeff didn't want to make it seem something between Bob Ford and himself, and this crowd was not going to be talked out of anything. He shouted at the limits of his voice: "All right, you dumb yahoos, but yuh-all are not puttin' this town up a tree . . . I just sent a telegram to Governor Bascom." Yank had joined him on the porch and Jeff growled at him: "Git the damn' thing goin'!"

149

Yank, stirred to action, grabbed his telegrapher's cap—one worn by train engineers with a little pasteboard sign bearing the title—and leaped to his station in front of the equipment to click away like a lunatic woodpecker. Unfortunately he was not getting any clacking in return. He thumped the sender as hard as he could, as if that would help bring a response.

Holding up the balance sheet given him earlier by Bowers so that it caught the light from one of the porch lanterns, Jeff announced in loud florid tones: "Y'all better hear this first. 'Dear Governor Bascom. Certain malefactors and transgressors in our town are threatening to lynch a citizen. This is illegal in Creede. Please send cavalry. Yuhrs for law an' order an' the future of our glorious state uh Colorado, yuhr ol' pard, Randolph Jefferson Smith.' "

It took a couple of minutes for the message to disseminate through that noisy, agitated crowd, but at length it began to quiet down.

A miner did call out tentatively: "The governor's hunnerts of miles away, Soapy. Why should we be scared of him?"

"You must be an outlander, friend, if yuh don't know our Bascom."

Frisco Red Harris still sat slumped, head down, on the patient mule, seconds from death if it moved. Soapy, looking over at him, took offense at his obvious despair. It bordered on disloyalty.

"Y'all hang 'round"—not that anyone was going anywhere—"we ought tuh be gettin' an answer enna minute now." Jeff darted an anxious look over his shoulder at Bowers, standing beside Yank. The Rev bolted inside.

"Enna minute now," Jeff persisted, trying to keep it positive. He spotted Kelly, trying to fire up enthusiasm for the hanging in some of the miners around him and thought he might use that for distraction. "Where's ol' Bob, Kelly? Where's he hidin' this time?"

Kelly shouted back that Bob didn't like to visit the low-class end of town, but got nothing for it.

Inside the Library, his corpulent figure jiggling and suffering, Bowers pounded up the stairs to the secret room. He jammed in his key and thrust the door open. There on the floor, surrounded by bottles large and small, lay Fatty, snoring loudly. Bowers pounced on him with great vigor for a man of his age and dimension. "Fatty! Fatty, wake up, god damn you. Get on the generator. Jeff's in trouble out there."

Half asleep, like a lamb to the slaughter, Fatty was led to climb aboard a stationary, tireless bicycle wired to a generator, hence to the "transmitter", and there he went to work. His eyes might be closed, but his mighty thighs pumped prodigious amounts of energy into the system.

Bowers plunked himself in front of the sender and frantically tapped the governor's response, or at least the noise required to suggest that there was a message coming in.

Out on the porch, Jeff heard the receiver *clacking* away and sighed with relief. "There it is, folks! Gather 'round."

Suddenly it went silent.

In the secret room, Bowers was almost as alarmed as Jeff. He looked over and saw that Fatty had fallen soundly asleep across the handlebars. Jumping up, he grabbed a Bible from a wall shelf and hit Fatty across the head with it. His victim instantly perked up, though his eyes remained closed, and began pumping again like mad. The Creede telegraph was up and working again.

Not wanting to take any more chances, Yank jumped up quickly, waving one of his scribble-filled pages. Jeff grabbed it out of his hand and peered out at his audience triumphantly.

"Here it is, boys, here it is. Let's see what the man y'all called Bloody-Boy Bascom in the last election . . . y'all think he got that name pluckin' pussywillas? . . . let's see what he has tuh say." Posturing a little, he sang out as in a stump speech: " 'Dear Jeff, pleased tuh hear from yuh. Desperate an' unAmerican situation in Creede I will fix. Lynching and progress will never mix.' " Jeff paused to give his telegrapher an evil look. Yank shrugged helplessly. " 'Will send on cavalry immediately. Yuhr friend, Governor David Bascom.' Well, now, do I call off those troopers?" He paused dramatically. "Or will there be a lot uh sour apples hangin' on that tree in a few days?"

The crowd began to stir—then disperse. He had pulled it off. Jeff longed to wipe away the sweat but not the slightest sign of weakness was allowed in such a situation, so he would wait for the wind to do its job.

The members of the Ford gang who had played such a large part in the affair were frustrated beyond endurance. Lev let the crowd melt around and away from him until he stood singularly alone, facing Jeff and his party up on the porch.

"Lev!" Kelly called, coming over. "Wait. I can't stand it. Him all the time talkin' us down. I'm gonna hang that bastard anyways!" He started toward the mule still holding up Frisco Red Harris.

Jeff stepped down off the porch, intercepting him. "Wait just a minute there, friend." At the same time he opened his coat wide to show an empty holster.

"Maybe I'll kill you first, sharper!" Lev shouted in his face, emotions clearly spiraling. He jerked his pistol and aimed it at Jeff's belly.

Kelly decided to hold back. Maybe Lev would do their work for them, after all.

Any hope Jeff had of getting close enough to take the man down without gunfire evaporated. He stopped in his tracks. "Yuh gonna shoot an unarmed man, mister?" He indicated what was left of the crowd. "They'll turn on yuh, I give yuh mah word on that. They'll enjoy hangin' yuh just as much as him."

"I don't care, I don't care no more, you cheap chiselin' high-binder. I'm sick of bein' shamed by you. I can't stand it no more. You don't have a pistol. 'Round here that's you bein' too dumb to go on livin', Soapy! What kind of a name's that for a man? You ain't no man, an' I'd just as soon settle you as a dog."

Jeff shouted back toward the Library: "Fatty! He shoots me, give him both barrels."

Lev laughed, or what he thought of as a laugh but would have sounded to anyone else like the devil giving another turn of the rack. "You diddled us once before. . . ."

Fatty wasn't the sort to wait for things to happen; he preferred to be the first. A shotgun roared twice, one barrel after the other, and blew Lev several feet back of where he had stood, his blood preceding his body, landing as a heap of rags in a little ring of rising dust. The blood and parts of him made a larger penumbra around what was well along toward being a corpse.

The remaining crowd was stunned into silence, but, when their motors got going again, they mostly ran like buckshot, fast and in all directions. The Ford gang didn't run, but they backed away uptown with weapons in their hands.

Jeff was disgusted. He walked over and looked down at the body. "God-damn' fool. Yuh had tuh have it, didn't yuh?"

Syd, Bowers, and Yank came over as well as some of the girls from the Library who showed a lively interest in corpses whenever they appeared, maybe as a result of their experiences with men generally. Unimpressed by all the noise and furor, the mule remained complacently under the tree, waiting for someone to hit or kick it into movement.

"Get Red off that damned mule," Jeff ordered impatiently of no one in particular. "Good thing it wasn't a horse, or he'd be wavin' in the wind."

"What do we do with him?" Syd asked.

"After yuh get the rope off his ignorant neck, give him a hundred dollars an' tell him tuh ride it on out uh here."

Yank and Bowers hurried over to the tree where Red remained seemingly ignorant of everything that had happened. When they got to him and asked him how he was, his only answer was a belch. As it turned out, he was very drunk, and, when they removed the noose, he fell off the mule. It finally walked away, apparently bored.

Jeff, regarding the whole scene, shook his head and spoke to Syd beside him: "Why can't they just let a man do a little quiet business? Ever'where we go it's the same god-damn' thing. Yuh watch, there'll be hell on the way."

Not hell but certainly trouble. The city council had given itself an office in the form of a large tent in the center of town with a large sign in front. The construction of a clapboard city hall went on next to it.

Jeff, who happened to be in a thankful Mattie's arms at the time, was asked politely by their messenger if he might not attend a meeting. More out of curiosity than anything, Jeff went. It was one in the morning.

"My hat's off to you, Smith," Moses said across the card table that served as a desk and through clouds of cigar smoke. Everyone except Jeff, who declined out of irritation, had a drink in front of them. By God, they looked prosperous and self-satisfied.

"I thought yuh were up guardin' yuhr mine?" Jeff said with asperity.

Moses took it well, with a chuckle real or forced. "Oh, hell, I can't afford to die . . . I'm too rich." He wasn't embarrassed, that was obvious.

"An' for the rest of yuh, I guess it's the same, huh?"

"You did a fine job, Jeff," Cameron assured him. "Don't spoil it now by goin' against us for being who we are. After all, there is a dead man in town now, shot down more or less from behind . . . I have to point that out."

"Used tuh be lots of 'em, an' this one happened to be tryin' tuh kill me. Yuh sayin' that's wrong?"

"No, no," Moses soothed. "I guess you had to. It isn't gonna make Bob Ford happy, though."

"No, he'd be a lot happier if the son-of-a-bitch had killed me. As long as we're pointin' things out, I was unarmed facin' that mob. Ennabody here got doubts about that."

"Not a bit," Moses said. "No need to be ruffled. We know it had to happen."

"What is it yuh want from me?"

"We don't want anything," Cameron assured him. "You've done it . . . established a new example of civic order. We can't argue with that."

"Except . . . ," Moses added with a wry smile, and everyone waited for him to finish the sentence, "except we feel you should have turned the criminal, that Red Harris, over to us. See, we're settin' up a court now and this thug did kill a man."

Jeff cut in: "I heard all about it. They were gamblin', words were exchanged, both drew. What did yuh want mah man tuh do, wave a fairy wand?"

"Ve hear different," Schumhaldter said. "Ve hear dis

Harris fella pulled out da gun first."

"It was a fair fight."

"A court might have decided that, Jeff," Warman said. "The point is we didn't have him to try."

"No fault uh yuhr own. I seem tuh remember I'm the one saved him from the rope. Y'all forget that?"

"The point is," the editor said, "then you let him go. Jeff, I've been your greatest supporter here, you know that. And it's not about to change, either, but we do need to take some steps toward a more legal way of settling disputes."

"It was self-defense," Smith said stubbornly.

"Jeff," Moses said more gently, "the other fella never fired a shot. Harris put six in him. You said you wanted law and order."

"An' we got it. I risked mah life tonight tuh give it tuh yuh." He paused to make sure this wasn't lost on anyone. "But I believe mah men. Anyhow, he's gone from here now, so what more do yuh want? Right now, I'm real tired, gentlemen. That standin' down a mob can take it right out of a fella."

He turned his back on them and walked out, headed for the warm, loving, thankful arms that awaited his embrace. Timed perfectly for the exit, they heard him say: "When yuh think on it, gentlemen, things are better for yuh here than they've ever been, an' y'all are makin' uh helluva lot uh money undisturbed by me."

They all remained sitting there in his wake and no one spoke for a while, although there were some grim expressions.

"Loyalty can be a grand thing," Moses observed a little sadly, "but in Jeff's case I'm afraid it's somebody's downfall . . . his or ours." That raised a chorus of agreement.

Chapter Seventeen

Whatever the muckety-mucks thought of his popularity and usefulness, Jeff now received enormous attention and praise around town for preventing the lynching, including from many who had been part of the mob. All over south Creede business flourished. Jeff even invested in another saloon, against Moses's advice, that straddled the line marking Bob's territory, claiming that growth and expansion were the American way. Besides, Ford didn't need it. His own business was terrible.

The Creede stock market was a brilliant success, as could be seen by events taking place in the headquarters room upstairs in the Library. Fatty and Bowers sat over a table, diligently drawing cards and recording the results first on paper, then an easel-mounted chalk board covered with names of corporations, the accompanying figures indicating that day's profit and loss.

Bowers drew a two of hearts. "Chrysler Wagons . . . down two." Another card, a four of diamonds: "American sugar . . . up four. Still a good buy, I reckon."

Fatty grunted and drew a card himself. "Danbury Corn products . . . down three," he mumbled.

Bowers stopped him. "Wait just a minute." He came over and looked at the cards on the table. "That's up."

"It ain't, neither," Fatty argued. "Clubs is up, spades is down."

"Soapy wants it up, anyhow. He's got it himself."

"Don't seem right. If the prices don't depend on the cards, what do they depend on?"

Yank entered the room and locked it behind him. "Got some new prices for me? Lot of buyers and sellers downstairs bitin' their lips."

Bowers handed him the sheets. "I'll get it on the telegraph."

"Say, that miner, Dundee, workin' the old Perkins claim, should I give him a boy or a girl?" Yank asked.

"Wha'd you give him the last time?" Fatty asked.

"Girl."

"Boy, keep it even."

"I need a name?"

"Jasper."

"Jasper!" Bowers said from over by the telegraph. "I wouldn't name a hog Jasper."

"Me, neither," Yank agreed, going over to look out the window.

Fatty took umbrage. "An' what's wrong with it? It's a fine, upstandin' American name. I don't see nothin' wrong with Jasper, no ways."

Bowers and Yank caught on and shared a look.

Fatty defied them to say anything more. "Well, there's nothin' wrong with it . . . fine manly name. . . ."

"Oh, oh," Yank said, glancing at the street below.

"What is it?" Bowers asked, not caring very much.

"Trouble. Come see for yourself."

Bowers got up and looked out. On the street, coming into town, were three ox-teams pulling wagons full of women and children.

"Think we should tell Soapy?" Yank wondered.

They didn't have to. Jeff was down on the street, welcoming the newcomers, shaking grimy hands, a one-man chamber of commerce and enjoying it.

"Yes, sir, we heard you got law and order here now and a man can do some prospectin' without worrying 'bout the wife and kids," said one of the new arrivals.

"Absolutely, my friend," Jeff assured him with a figurative wink toward the Library. "And have a little fun on the side."

The man grinned, and his wife wondered why.

At times like this Soapy's boys wondered just exactly who was Randolph Jefferson Smith. Not only that, but two days later there was a church raising for the pastor Jeff had defended and helped along. The Bible-thumper was rising in the world of Creede lately, up from a leaky tent to a real wooden building with a tin roof. It was a wondrous construction, more or less round. "That way, the devil can't get us in a corner," the pastor explained cheerfully, so that Jeff couldn't tell if he was serious. Nevertheless, Soapy was in attendance for the celebration and also encouraged his boys to "sermonize" there.

Bowers was invited and delivered a sermon that, even as it inspired, also bewildered everyone who heard it. Opinions varied widely as to its content and source, and some people spent days trying to find anything at all from the Bible that might have sanctioned it. Canada Bill spoke on the evil of cards, especially three-card monte, a game invented by Satan himself. Jeff gave a talk on his favorite theme: that the way of the transgressor is hard to change. Soapy seldom explained himself, but he did call what he was doing "public relations" and said he was trying to establish something lasting here. He just didn't spell out exactly what.

If this was a downward path for Soapy, the slide became more precipitous. He decided that Creede had to have a school for the few kids who were around now. Collecting in the usual manner, by cajolery and implied menace, it became more than a promise. In fact, the subscription was so popular that even people in the north end of town contributed. But not Bob Ford, not this time. He had heard by how much Soapy had topped him on the church fund raiser and wasn't subjecting himself to that kind of double-cross again. He denounced it as a swindle and told the hat-passer to get out of his saloon or he would shoot him for trespassing. A substantial building went up on the edge of town without his help and was painted bright red. It even had a large bell in front until somebody stole it. All that was needed was a teacher. That turned out to be more difficult than erecting the building itself. Advertisements were placed in the Denver papers, but Creede's reputation had spread at least that far and no single young woman was willing to risk it. A couple came and looked, and fled.

Soapy Smith, the man who hated losing, cobbled together a ramshackle program. Some of the instruction was done by the few "respectable" and literate women of the town, including a couple of the new mothers. Mattie taught French and took it very seriously, going so far as to acquire a quieter wardrobe through a catalog, or what she thought was quieter, since the kids found it quite lively. Fortunately she knew a lot about discipline.

The pastor told Bible stories and lessons. Bowers, very good with figures, taught some math. Yank, who had always claimed to be a direct descendent of the famed New England theologian, Jonathan Edwards, talked about the history of that region and speechifying in general. He owned a book of famous speeches and had found it useful in his chosen occupation for drawing crowds.

But somehow people got tired of the steady beat of obligation and kids are always ready to get tired of school unless someone drives them to it. Besides, their parents had other work for them. Eventually the schoolhouse stood forlorn and empty. Jeff's friends and associates, even Mattie, soon found it best not to mention the subject in his presence.

The town might be relatively quiet and most things, certainly commerce of every sort, appeared to be going smoothly for a while, but one of Soapy's favorite barroom aphorisms was: "The defeated can afford to sleep easy. The victorious can't afford to sleep at all." He was right and the better for knowing it. At three one morning he lay in Mattie's embrace in her quarters on the second floor of the bordello. She slept deeply and quietly, but he didn't sleep at all—some instinct. It was too quiet outside, too peaceful, too harmless. Horses, mules, and oxen never shut up, but where were the drunks, the screaming whores, the losers at the table?

He heard what he thought was a boot step on the outside stairway where he had taken the precaution of spreading some broken glass. There followed scraping, crunching sounds, enough to set off a major alarm. Jeff's pistol hung on the bedpost as was customary, but the noisemaker was close by, and Jeff wasn't sure he had time to go for it, not and protect Mattie at the same time.

Another sound, right at the open window, told the rest. Jeff grabbed Mattie around the waist and, in a single sweeping thrust, barreled them both off of the bed onto the hard floor. She let out a scream that overlay and almost swallowed the three gunshots that came in to chew up the pillow and sheets. Smoke hung in the window frame as if in a painting, then came the sound of scrambling footsteps.

Mattie went on screaming and cursing, trying to orient herself while Jeff grabbed his pistol, leaped to the window, naked, and got off three shots of his own down the stairway, shouting: "Yuh spineless son-of-a-bitch, yuh back-shooting pile uh horseshit . . . !" He could make out some wooden splinters flying off the wooden railing and the shape of a man as he hit the dirt and ran.

Then Mattie was trying to pull him away from the window, yelling that she didn't want to be a widow before she was even married.

"Yuh got tuh get rid uh these god-damn' backsteps, honey," Jeff grumbled when she had quieted down.

Stubborn and inappropriate as ever, she chose this unlikely moment to argue. "A woman in my profession needs one. It's expected." In the back of her mind, of course, was the idea of spreading a little jealousy. "Anyhow, you used it enough."

"How 'bout a rope ladder? You know, Rumpelstiltskin."

That made her smile and got her back into bed, where they looked to do some more horizontal dancing with the both of them wide awake now that the blood was very high and running fast.

In the aftermath, not much was made of the attempt since any one of a thousand people, besides Ford's bunch, might have tried it over some lost game or bunco. Jeff swore not to sleep in front of any more open windows. But next morning there was another incident when one of Soapy's men buffaloed a townsman in a dispute over a girl, cracking his skull.

Holy Moses, strolling down to the Library where Jeff was to be found most days, saw a miner leap from the porch and run through town shouting: "It's a boy, a boy! Name's Jasper! Ain't it great?" Yank was leaning an elbow on the telegraph table, grinning like a proud parent.

Holy wasn't in a grinning mood but he couldn't repress a

slight smile at the sight of the ecstatic new father running so disjointedly. Jeff had been asked to come to the council tent and had refused, so here was Moses come to meet him and deliver their complaint.

Having so narrowly avoided the Grim Reaper the night before, Smith was in a less than giving mood. He marched out of the Library and down to meet his accuser in the midst of the dusty street where everyone could see or hear. Convinced that by now he held the citizenry in his palm, it suited him to have the confrontation in public.

Holy expressed his relief that Jeff had survived the assassination attempt by person or persons. . . .

"Holy, yuh know damn' well it was one uh Ford's men."

"I will when I see the evidence on it."

"Where's the rest of our brave council?"

"Where they ought to be, working. We all work, you know. Having different hours than yourself."

Jeff let it slide and Moses went on to tell how they had arrested one of his men, Dolly Brooks—Bat had anyway—and he was being held in the new jail.

"I didn't even know we had one. Not a real one."

"Didn't yesterday, do now."

"Progress," Jeff said in his best laconic style.

"We think so."

"See here," Jeff said, "this is a rough town on both sides uh the bar, Holy, so don't ask me tuh break down an' cry over some poor bastard got his head stomped. He's still kickin', isn't he? Anyways, I heard the story an' it was uh fair fight. I want my man released."

"We hoped you'd see reason."

"I'll ask the boys to be more temperate."

"Not good enough."

"No, I had a hunch it wouldn't be."

163

"Jeff, you got men here wanted on charges in Denver an' a lot of other places. The council feels they should leave town. We had a meeting last night. Half of Creede was there."

"Didn't bother yuh before."

"We weren't a town before."

"I'm wanted on many of those same charges, Holy."

"We're willing to make an exception."

"The exception y'all are gonna make is lettin' Dolly go." The rare, pugnacious look came into Jeff's black eyes. "I don't want tuh have to come get him. And tell Bat I'd like to see him." No more discussion, he turned on his heel like the colonel he had impersonated in the past and stalked back into the Library.

Moses, left standing alone, the object of a hundred stares, summoned all his dignity and walked solemnly in the opposite direction.

Bat came to see Jeff at his office within the hour. He had anticipated the object of their meeting, bringing a slightly damaged, very grateful Dolly Brooks with him.

"Jeff, I can't do this any more," he said, sitting and sipping Smith's best bourbon. "I arrest someone and you release him. Puts me right in the middle. Especially when he deserves to be arrested. I understand your point, but it's not right for me. I'm either sheriff or I'm not, and I never much took to the job, anyhow. I've been offered a chance to promote some fights up in Ogden and I'm gonna take it. I hope there's no hard feelings."

"Oh, hell, no." Jeff jumped up quickly and gave Masterson a warm handshake. "We're ol' pards. Yuh know that." He even tried to press some hundred-dollar bills on him— Soapy never counted money—but they were refused, Bat saying that he had done real well here.

"Dolly gave me a little bit of trouble and it shows on him."

"I have no doubt he deserved it an' worse. Thanks for ever'thin', Bat. Our paths will cross."

Still, it made Jeff a little sad when Masterson was gone. One thing Jeff had always been good at in the past was seeing writing when it appeared on walls, and the auguries were finally there again and some kind of drastic action seemed called for.

The next day Yank sat on the porch by his telegraph key, waiting for customers. Syd stood in the bordello doorway, lazily puffing on his pipe. Bowers, as was his noonish habit, snoozed in a high-backed straw chair nearby, while a cheap cigar burned slowly through his fingers. Fatty likewise dozed, filling to overflowing a groaning glider next to Bowers. It was a peaceful picture all around.

"There goes Soapy," Yank observed, in the manner of small town loafers, as Jeff rode past on his way out of town. He waved at the boys on the porch.

"Where's he going?" Syd asked, slurring the words a little.

"Off to send a telegram," he said.

Fatty woke up at that. "Why don't he send it from here? . . . oh."

Another thing that Jeff had often opined when bellied up to a bar was that the secret of his success was talking optimistically and thinking pessimistically. It wasn't quite true in that he often succumbed to his own dreams and illusions, but the more eloquently he put them forth, the more he was prepared to believe them. What the wall writing said this time around was that he had better eliminate the major competition soon if he hoped to continue his rule of Creede. He knew the townspeople liked to let others do their fighting and play off their enemies against each other. He had seen it. They never seemed to share for long his view that there was room for everyone in this world, even the honest sharper.

The messages to be sent were already written, crammed into his back pocket. They were going to several newspapers in Missouri, including the perfectly respectable *Post-Dispatch* in St. Louis. He knew journalism and how it could be used through gossip columns. He should. He had manipulated gossip columns himself to a fare-thee-well in Denver.

Soapy's items were all about a man named Bob Ford who never stopped bragging everywhere he went about shooting Jesse James and getting away with it, how he regaled whole audiences with his stories while getting rich in Creede, Colorado. He was, no doubt, doing a lot better than anyone in that miserable little red-dirt band of robbers and thieves he had once called comrades, but who tried to bring him down after he had rid the country of one of the foulest, meanest, *etc*. Why Ford was practically king of the state now, according to these missives. Soapy knew how to lay it on.

It didn't take long to see the effect. Shortly after he returned to his stand-off with the self-appointed leading citizens and a period of relative tranquility, the balance went topsy-turvy.

Bob Ford was sleeping in his office/apartment one night, his arm around a little whore named Rita who had never heard of Jesse James and was one of the few who answered to his blandishments these days. It was three o'clock in the morning and the streets in the north end had emptied. A warm summer night with a breeze teasing the curtains meant open windows. Then the demon that had haunted Bob Ford for ten years crept into his dreams:

> Oooh, Jesse had a wife
> He loved her all his life
> The children they were brave,
> when that dirty little coward,
> shot down Mister Howard
> and put our Jesse in his grave. . . .

It wasn't bad enough that the voice was distinctly Southern, but also strange in the hearing, far away and yet somehow close, almost eerie in its lamenting evocation of distant hills, trails, and times. It was also a song that simply was not sung in public, not in Creede or anywhere else where Bob Ford held sway. The penalty had always been death.

It jolted Bob out of his sleep and onto his feet in one alarmingly eruptive jack-in-the-box movement, one that knocked the poor whore right out of bed as he leaped for his pistols on the post and then to the window. Leaning so far out in his attempt to see, he almost fell two stories to the ground. The voice was somehow, almost miraculously it seemed to him, far away now. There was no one on the street.

> Oh, hear of Jesse's wife
> Made a mourner all her life. . . .

The voice became fainter and slowly disappeared. Ford threw the bewildered Rita out of the room with no little roughness and got back into bed to pull the sheets over himself, shivering. By dawn the linen might as well have spent the night under water.

At sunrise, there was Bob, with some of the staff, boarding up the windows and eventually the front entrance of Ford's

167

Exchange while the town's idlers got an early start on their loafing, watching all this excitement unfold. When the job was done, the workmen having disappeared so that it was safe, one of the old men got up and threw a stone against the door. It was an act of such heroism that it made his fellows cackle like naughty boys.

Chapter Eighteen

Reports reached Jeff about a small pack of well-armed new-comers, lean, hard-faced riders used to back roads and bad times, hanging around Creede in the aftermath of Ford's panicky flight. They had little contact with the townspeople or its entertainment palaces, didn't seem to have enough money for the gang to bother with, and beyond that they minded their own business, mostly staying out of town. If they ran up any bills, they paid them promptly. But they were always looking, looking for something or someone. The odd thing was that no one ever saw any of them smile. Jeff said to let them be.

The mystery of where their former dictator had gone ab-sorbed the conversation—barroom, dinner table, or camp-fire—of all of Creede. And what about that spectral singer of the forbidden song? Everyone had heard about that. People claimed to have seen him, but no two could describe him in the same way. Perhaps it was one of that bunch of newcomers who had no interest in mining yet stayed around, doing nothing. It was all very strange. Could it have been Frank James himself who sang that song, or even the ghost of Jesse, come for his revenge?

No one believed Ford was gone from Creede for good, al-though maybe Jeff and some of his gang wanted it to be so. But Bob was pretty much out of places to run for one thing, and the isolation here was perfect for a man with his history. Besides, it wasn't his temperament to run, any more than it would have been for a wolverine in heat. Rumors abounded that he was still recruiting shooters and had taken his treasure with him into the mountains, some place where he could re-coup, re-equip, and plot his revenge.

Holy Moses was observed standing in the street one day with several of the newly expanded town council around him, all of them jabbering, looking and pointing up into the high country with great portent. Holy seemed to know, like he knew everything else, that Ford was up there somewhere. On that particular occasion he ended by shaking his head and looking distinctly glum, after which they all looked glum.

Jeff refused to worry and the gang was too busy making money and carrying on as only they knew how to do. Swindling people was their happiness and their religion, their food and drink, and they were seated at a very rich table. Imagine, a whole town to plunder, a tolerant boss, and mostly they got to make their own rules! Bat's replacement as sheriff was seventy-five years old and half blind. Such opportunities didn't come along very often in a grifter's life.

Standing out on a balcony of the Library, arms around each other, wearing no more than was needed to fend off the cold of that late hour, Mattie and Jeff watched a display of heat lightning up in the mountains. Mattie said Bob was up there, all right. What they were seeing was one of his typical tantrums.

Holy came to the Tivoli to have another talk with Jeff about the town's future. He had to admit that the council's plans, with Smith's gang holding sway down here and the threat of a Ford return hanging over their heads from up there—he pointed at the ceiling, as if Ford might come from heaven—well, they were in a trough. It was, he hinted, a kind of last chance for both of them.

"Bring Mister Moses an' me a bottle uh that French champagne," Jeff called to the bartender, "the good stuff! And some ceegars."

"One thing I need to know, Jeff . . . there's some new boys hanging around town, reports don't always agree, three, six . . . I don't know. Tough-lookin' bunch."

"I've seen 'em."

"They're not part of your outfit?"

"Nope."

"You had any doin's with 'em?"

"They don't socialize much. Come in for a drink sometimes, play a game, look 'round, pay up, disappear. They're nothin' tuh me, Holy. Don't trouble us, we don't trouble them."

"They've been known to ask about Mister Ford," Holy mused, his tone and look wry. "Maybe we shouldn't draw too much from it, but one was heard to be hummin' 'The Bonny Blue Flag'." He couldn't help himself. He had to snigger at his own obviousness.

"That so?" Jeff said, unconcerned and uninvolved. "Well, that's Bob's affair . . . wherever he is." He lit both of their cigars while the bartender poured the champagne.

"You know, you could do right well here, Jeff. It's gonna be a great town and you could go right along with it. Even the railroad might be coming in."

"No disrespect, Holy, but I heard that 'bout every little pip-squeak town I've ever been in. Gonna be New York City someday, they tell yuh, an' they believe it, too. But when the silver or gold runs out, there's nothin' left there but a pile uh rocks and some good amount uh wreckage, human an' otherwise. We may not be much, but we're still smarter than most of 'em. We move on."

"That what you're gonna do here?"

"No. I have tuh admit, I kind uh like it here. It's cozy, and lucrative. Maybe yuh're right, it will be New York City someday. New York uh the Rockies, ennahow." He grinned and shook his head.

"You're a cut above your profession, Jeff, got some education somewhere, lot of style. People like you. Go ahead and marry Mattie, why don't you . . . settle down. Been plenty in her profession got to be royalty in England. Just give up what you're doing, that's all we ask, the sporting life."

"Sorry. I got mah boys to think uh. They look up tuh me. Anyways, there's got to be a place in the world for sharpers tuh make a livin' like ever'body else . . . might as well be here."

Holy moved his polished boot back and forth along the brass foot rail beneath the bar's overhang. It was as close as he ever got to showing nerves.

"You're out of step, Jeff. Just like Bob Ford was."

"Poor old Bob. I guess we 'spected y'all tuh be grateful for that."

"We were."

"For a week or so."

Holy looked sad. He stared down at where his foot was leaving a polish streak on the rail. "I like you, Jeff."

"Aw, hell, I like yuh, too, Holy. We're just cut out uh different cloth, is all."

The loving that night was terrific. Jeff Smith thought maybe he was the luckiest man in the world, but then he had never been so keenly attuned to women's sensibilities that he might have recognized the element of desperation in the fire that Mattie had stoked. No, like smoke and talk, liquor and late hours, card games and deadly games, women were just a part of his life, but they weren't the whole.

172

Mattie, in a peignoir, was freshening up in front of the mirror on her dresser, something she did often. Jeff, damp and exhausted, was still naked, recovering on the bed, an absent smile on his face—unwarranted, as it turned out.

"I haven't had a good night's sleep since we started getting rich," Mattie said, watching him in the mirror. "What is it about money that makes men so randy?"

"It isn't the money, sweetheart, it's the gettin' it off the other fella."

"Most of the time someone's getting it off of you. Honest to God, if you're gonna play faro and lose, the least you could do was play in your own establishment so you're only losing to yourself."

"Where'd be the fun in that? Yuh might also have mentioned I like helpin' people. I do a lot uh that."

She turned and looked at him with an unusual tenderness, that thing women do sometimes before they tear loose. "I know it," she said, "and it's what I love about you." Her voice steeled somewhat. "Only do you have to give away so damn' much? Honest to God, Jeff, sometimes I think you need a keeper."

He missed the import of that reference, too.

She went back to her refitting, running a gold comb through all that long near-gold hair. "What's this about Moses talkin' so serious with you today?" She didn't miss much.

"Thinks we ought tuh retire, yuh an' me. I told him we're havin' too much fun." He threw himself back to lie flat and stare at the ornate ceiling where generations of chubby angels had watched the unangelic things going on below and apparently, from their expressions, enjoyed them.

"Maybe you ought to've listened to him," she said with deceptive matter-of-factness.

"Honey, we're just startin'. I've sent for more uh the boys. This is a chance of a lifetime here."

She turned on him suddenly, twisting in her chair to glare at him. "You never learn, do you? Always waiting around for people's gratitude when they're never grateful. No one is. It's dog eat dog. And someday you'll wait too long."

"Well, now, that's a mite cynical toward me, darlin'."

"I know. Down deep, you believe. Always waiting for someone to elect you king or something."

"Well, now, sweetheart," he said mildly, "I've always thought in another time or place I might have been one uh them. I'm equipped, I believe, by nature tuh take on responsibility. Now how about yuh let me take care uh Moses and you take care uh me." He reached out his arms to her.

Her answer was to throw a perfume bottle at him and yell: "No! No, sir, no more of that!"

"Whoaaa, horse. What's got inta yuh?"

"Not until you marry me."

"Speakin' uh horses, that one's kind uh been out uh the barn for a while, hasn't it?"

"I don't care, Jeff. I'm going to have everything I told you . . . marriage, respectability. . . ." She got up and came to sit on the edge of the bed, softening her look and voice. "Between us we got plenty of money, or at least I do, and I'll go anywhere. San Francisco. . . ." She wound down, knowing by the relentless neutrality on his face that she was not reaching him.

Without rancor, when she longed for rancor, he said: "Yuh do what yuh got tuh, hon. I wouldn't ever try tuh stop yuh."

She was biting off her words now. "It comes down to whether you love me or not."

Jeff sighed and sat up, pulling the sheet over his nakedness

174

out of respect for the serious turn the conversation had taken. "I guess maybe I do . . . or I wouldn't tell yuh this. Mattie, I'm married."

In shock, she yelled: "Married? You?"

"Hey, now, yuh wanted tuh marry me yuhrself a minute ago."

She stared at him, unbelieving. "You bastard," she said finally.

"Yuh 'member that little singer come tuh Denver with the opera company? Addie Nelson? At the time I believe it was what yuh're talkin' 'bout, wantin' to be kind uh . . . normal and, yeah, respectable. Got a son, though, back in Saint Louie. I kept 'em out of it."

"You rotten son-of-a-bitch, all this time. . . ."

"I'm sorry, Mattie. Even most uh the gang don't know."

"I killed a man for you!"

She threw it right in his face. He couldn't blame her for being angry. The fact that he really did care for her obviated any notion of anger on his part. In a lame attempt at lightness, he said: "I thought that was for love. I didn't know it was for marriage."

Mattie went to the closet and pulled out a coat, angrily throwing it on over her peignoir. Jeff watched in silent consternation. When she came back to stand over him, looking down at him like a blonde Medea with well-combed hair, she announced: "Well, here's how I feel about it, Mister Smith. When someone cuts your throat or empties a whole six rounds into your worthless gizzard, causin' a real painful death, I'll hire an orchestra for everyone who wants to dance on your grave and I'll lead the terpsichore."

"Holy Toledo, you women sure. . . ."

Mattie was already headed for the door, a fury in flight.

"Mattie, hold on, now!"

She was gone, slamming the door hard enough behind her to stir the building.

"This is *yuhr* place!" Finally, out of sheer perplexity, he picked up one of his boots and threw it against the door.

Mattie was the same unconstrained fury with the wind blowing the tails of her coat as she stomped down the filthy street in her mules, straight to the council's tent headquarters. Throwing aside the flap and entering, she found it empty except for Holy Moses, sleeping on a cot, the candle on the table next to him having burned down to a nub, a fallen Bible on the floor. She shook him roughly. "Holy, wake up, damn you."

He awoke, scrambling for the pistol under his pillow.

"It's me, Mattie! Don't shoot me, for Lord's sake!"

He sat up slowly, rubbing his eyes, and placed the pistol carefully on the table. "Shouldn't never come in on a man when he's sleeping."

"You can't very well knock on a tent, can you?"

He lit a lamp and, preparing to stand so he could put on his pants, suggested she turn around. Her exasperated look told him just how foolish that was.

"I see your point," he told her, and started getting dressed. "I don't reckon you come over here out of fatal attraction, anyway."

Mattie took a deep breath. "What would you do if I told you there wasn't any telegraph?"

There was a look so fierce on the usually imperturbable face of Moses that Mattie couldn't have imagined it. For a moment they both stopped moving.

But for him the struggle for self-control was over so swiftly that within seconds he was able to ask, while bringing his galluses up over his shoulders, in a perfectly even voice:

"That what you're tellin' me?"

She began to stalk back and forth, as much as that cramped space allowed, working up her own rage. "Damn him. I want everyone to know. I'm gonna tell this whole lousy town. I'm just gonna rub his face in the dirt for the way he. . . ."

She wasn't looking at anything except the wooden planks beneath her restless feet, but Moses was very close to her, and, when he barked the word—"No!"—she jumped back. "No, you're not," he said more quietly.

Madder still at being ambushed, she snapped—"Who says?"—and glared right back at him. "Who's gonna stop me?"

She started to storm out of the tent, but he grabbed her wrist with a hand that had done a lifetime of digging, and it hurt. She struggled to get loose but the look in his eyes discouraged any more violent gestures.

"My way is always to try to be reasonable, talk things out. That's why I liked Jeff. He's a gentleman that way. But now I'm giving you an order. Not one word to anyone. I can't be more plain."

He felt the sass go out of her and released her.

In a small, somewhat regretful voice, she asked: "What are you gonna do?"

"We'll take care of it."

Chapter Nineteen

With the eastern sky just beginning to redden and birds singing their fool heads off, Moses, Cameron, Schumhaldter, and newly enrolled councilmen rode tentatively through densely wooded high country, following an active stream. While they went, each stared into the shallow but turbulent depths as if it might contain the secret of life.

Every now and then, one of them would dismount, wade into the freezing water, shuddering, and pull the cable far enough out to show to the others. Twice they had to stop, hastily build a fire, and thaw out the volunteer to avoid frostbite. But motivation was high, the rage of emperors being nothing to that of a shopkeeper's feelings at being diddled, and they endured. Still, the line seemed to go on and on until a couple of the party wanted to give it up, arguing that no confidence men would ever be this industrious. Holy said they didn't know Jeff Smith very well or they wouldn't say that. He had no doubts himself.

His hard-headedness was rewarded finally. One of the party was riding through the water, running the cable through his hands when all of a sudden it jerked loose, left the streambed, went boldly up onto the shore, and there ended its exhaustive odyssey, tied off flagrantly to a humble birch tree.

"There it is, boys," Holy said, pointing to it, "the terminus of the Creede telegraph!" Then, while the others scowled or growled, the horses sensing the anger, snorting and pawing the ground, Moses started to laugh. He laughed until he had to wipe the tears from his eyes. The others, men who characteristically found nothing amusing about the human condition, stared at him mordantly.

Someone asked: "What's the joke?"

It was drizzling up in the mountains about ten miles north of Creede where Ford's gang had taken refuge in a small grouping of fur trappers' cabins. The buildings themselves were crumbling, leaking, and smelling of mold and animal waste so the increasingly large group of men, over twenty now, did most of their living out-of-doors. Every one of them was bored, restless, scratchy as well as uncomfortable. Bob kept them there by claiming that there were just a few more shooters coming in and that they needed numbers to go against a whole town where Soapy Smith was practically king.

Ford would add tales of the loot for the having when they did go back. Kelly and those from the original bunch could affirm that there were fortunes to be made off of Soapy Smith's bunch alone, and with all the silver in Creede they would be millionaires, the envy of everyone in the West—put the James' gang, Youngers, Daltons, all to shame.

A group was sitting hunched in ponchos or horse blankets around a sputtering fire two nights after the discovery that the telegraph was a fake. Down there it was still a secret from everyone but the council, and up here nothing of such goings-on was known to anyone. Bob Ford separated himself from the rest, sitting off to one side, brooding and nursing a whiskey bottle. Among criminals sullenness sometimes works as a mystique.

Bitter Creek Johnson, rain dripping off his tangled beard, was telling a tale. "I 'member, a bunch of us, I think we'd robbed a bank . . . yep, that was it, a bank. Or was it an assay office? Anyways, we come across that there Staked Plains in August. I tell you, it was root little hog or die. Hotter'n Hades, no food, no water. Had us this Indian guide who promised he knew the way. He didn't, an', oh, how we suffered. Hungry? I never been so hungry. . . ."

Finally some veteran of a thousand such campfire tales asked with a modicum of interest: "What happened?"

"We ate him."

No one said anything after that.

"Oncet," Bitter Creek began again, but this time was interrupted by the cry—"Rider comin' in!"—whereupon he instantly lost his audience. Everyone was on their feet, armed and ready.

It turned out to be Holy Moses. He rode slowly into the camp right up to the fire without saying anything, dismounted before a dozen pairs of feral eyes, all catching the light. Nonchalantly he warmed his hands, rubbing them together, and finally said—"Howdy!"—right and left while showing a slight smile that seemed to imply he had the upper hand here. He knew Bob Ford was in the gloom somewhere, watching, making a jackal's judgment of him as to threat or advantage. " 'Evenin', Bob."

"Holy."

Moses turned and strolled over to where Ford, rifle across his knees, was crouched down like a wild animal in an act of nature. "What if I was to tell you there wasn't any telegraph?"

Bob grunted, thought about it, and came as close to a grin as he had ever come.

Earlier that same day, Jeff had made an attempt to reach out to Mattie, but she refused to see him. In fact, one of the soiled doves quoted her as saying that, if she did see him, it would only be to put a bullet through his heart.

He was more upset by the breakup with Mattie than he would admit even to himself. It stayed on his mind all that day. He was forced to admit to himself that he really did love her, more than he could afford. But knowing her temper, he couldn't see her coming around any time soon, either. If it hadn't exactly broken his heart, surely it had badly bruised it. He had always feared the distraction of women, and here it was.

Anyway, there was the business to think about. He had noted—his gang was everywhere, depending as they did on good intelligence for all their scams—that Holy Moses and some of his faction had returned from a long morning ride the day before, looking worn and spent but not unhappy. Later, there was talk of an intense meeting in a private room in the back of the Diamond Café. It was obvious to Jeff that they felt secrecy was too vital for a tent.

None of this worried him overmuch, since he thought he still had a handle on things and could ride out whatever storm these good people of the shops and mines threw at him. This was his time. He might have to bring in some more boys of the tougher breed, although he didn't want to.

That afternoon the weather went through some strange peregrinations, cold one minute, warm the next, and finally settling on an oppressive, almost tropical, humidity that lay over the town for a couple of hours, pressing it farther down into its crevice between the mountains. Later, little bursts of vicious wind joined the big clouds piling up. These changed colors several times, eventually blackened, and finally delivered a good-size rain and blow that flattened a couple of Creede's flimsy buildings and tents. It was the precursor of those drizzles and showers that would make sodden Ford's encampment through the night.

181

As with all gamblers, Jeff was burdened with a certain amount of superstition, but nothing like the norm in his profession. He thought of himself as fundamentally logical and sensible and was seldom even aware of the weather, much less would he allow it to give him a chilly feeling along the spine. He tried to shake it off, even drinking more and talking louder than usual, but he became increasingly agitated so that some of his people noticed.

The gang, being mainly city people, was less adroit in reporting on those half-dozen strangers, riders all, who had slipped in and out of town without fuss or notice. Jeff thought he knew, but still he wondered, and wished he knew more.

Then at five o'clock he received a note from the hand of the same adolescent boy who had brought him news of the planned lynching. The kid seemed to be everywhere lately. Spelling and syntax were so crude as to make it difficult to read, but Jeff got most of it. Some strangers, newcomers to town, would appreciate his taking supper—**a plain meal**—with them around six that evening at their encampment. Their purpose, they said, was merely to **git to know u** and **learn the real facts**. It added: **We are ruf men but we are sutherners and gentlmen. Yur safty is promis.** It was signed—**Ed Dooley**—and a primitive map was attached. Maybe on a normal day, if one ever showed up, Jeff would not have answered such a risky summons, but the very lack of ease he was feeling, along with a certain amount of curiosity, were precisely what did prod him out into the countryside alone in a darkening rainstorm. He went the short distance, not long after Holy Moses had set out on his errand, and arrived at a small, tree-surrounded meadow carved out of the mountains a mile or so from town. As he approached, he heard gunfire that spooked his horse a bit and gave Jeff himself some second thoughts.

He rode on, anyway, through the trees, conscious that he was being watched, into a clearing where the shooting turned out to be merely target practice with rifles. He could only glance at it in passing, touching his hat politely, but his impression was of good marksmanship. Most target practice that Jeff witnessed had to do with pistols. Any kid fresh out of New York could get a big hat, put a pistol, or better two, on his hip, and call himself dangerous. When you had lasted as long as Smith, you knew they were only good for saloons, as he had so effectively demonstrated himself in recent days—you couldn't shoot far or hit much with them and serious shooters did their work with rifles.

Dooley, apparently the leader of the band, greeted him by the campfire, which was under a lean-to and flared brightly even in the fine rain. Jeff moved closer and began the serious work of drying off. The stranger was of a type, a thin, raw-boned, tall man with the kind of scars and weathering one expected, his skin so sun-blackened it shone even here in the storm and gloom.

Jeff noticed other things about this bunch: they had been around a long time, they were not young, and a lot of the hard things they had seen shown in their eyes. Still, Dooley and his friends, the silent sort mostly, greeted him with a kind of Southern courtliness.

When Jeff asked why he had been summoned, Dooley drawled: "Well, we heard things 'bout yuh. Yuh was a Southern man, lak us, fer one."

He waited for Jeff to fill in the blanks, and he did, smiling. "Noonen in the great state of Georgia, by way of Texas."

"Noonen," one of the men piped up, drawing closer to the fire as bacon and beans sizzled in the pan giving off their familiar odor, "I been by there, or mighty close. Fact is, I rode

183

with uh feller from close by it, I do believe. Abercrombie . . . somethin' Abercrombie."

Jeff, wise to the ways of these men, assured him that he might well have known someone by that name, although he had left Noonen while fairly young.

"There . . . I thought he might know him," the man, the youngest of the lot, said to the others, well pleased. He rubbed his gnarled, rein-roughened hands together.

A discussion of the many virtues of Georgia and the Southern states generally followed while they ate.

"Also," Dooley said at last, "we got the drift yuh was the kind uh feller knew things, knew people 'round this here area and where they was an' might be thinkin' uh doin'. See, we-all are lookin' for un old frien' uh ours . . . name uh Bob Ford."

"I know Bob," Jeff said.

"Figured yuh did," one of the others said. "He a friend uh yuhrs, too?"

Jeff laughed. "Same way he's a friend uh yuhrs."

There was some doubt for a moment among the group as to how to take that, but Dooley understood and almost smiled. "Don't know where we-all'd find our frien', do yuh? See, nobody in that town'll talk 'bout him. Got ever'body scairt, I reckon. We heerd yuh wasn't scairt uh much."

"What's yuhr business with Bob?"

Dooley shrugged. "Visit about ol' times, is all."

"I'm 'fraid I don't know where he is. I 'spect some folks do, but they haven't let me in on it. Got their own reasons for that."

"Yuh reckon he'll come back? See, we got kin an' chores an' things down home tuh care fer."

Jeff had to admit that he had no idea. "A licked dog generally goes lookin' for a smaller dog tuh pick on."

They looked at each other around that fire, faces sad and grave. A couple of them shook their heads, no, and Dooley took that as a decision. "That there's real disappointin'. See, we been havin' some discouragin' talk 'mongst us. Some uh the boys want tuh git back home, and I was hopin' yuh'd know. Y'all was our last chance, so tuh speak." He looked to his partners in this. "Don't see as how we got no choice. Jist missed the sum'bitch, damn his evil hide. God'll have to do it fer us. Kin's first."

They weren't any more disappointed than Jeff, who now wished that he had lied and insisted that Bob would be back any minute. He had always had trouble with lying outside the grift. It might not have made any difference since they were the sort who decided an issue impulsively and acted upon it, no matter what—it went a long way toward explaining Coffeeville and Northfield. As Jeff was leaving, Dooley apologized for bringing him all the way out there in the rain.

"Wouldn't have anybody here'bouts likely tuh be writin' tuh down home 'bout Bob, would yuh?" he asked politely. "Maybe some newspaper type uh fella?"

Jeff assured him that he didn't know anyone like that, and rode off, thinking that these people might have been a touch more subtle than he had given them credit for. Well, it was a wasted evening and a blown ploy, a lot of work for nothing. If Ford did come back, he would have to think of something else.

By morning the rain had stopped and the sun struggled to assert itself. Everything needed drying off, including Jeff himself. When he got out and around, it seemed the whole town had caught his mood of the day before, yet he couldn't quite put his finger on why he felt that to be the case.

By mid-afternoon he knew. The rumor was being spread:

"Bob Ford's coming down." Not only that, but Ford had a hundred killers with him and intended to make Creede pay for its support of Soapy Smith against him. When he had had his revenge, he would take over again and run things to his pleasure. Jeff suspected the council was behind the rumors and that it was merely a device to get him to move on. He had heard these types of stories in every frontier boom town he had been in, but they were for people with big mouths and soft bellies, for followers when he was a leader. He would dismiss them. Besides, what was he supposed to do, send for some cannon?

That was before he heard some of his men were slipping out of town. Canada Bill—all right—he was an invitee whose regular bailiwick was the plush club cars of intercontinental trains and had probably never fired a gun—but also Dolly Brooks, the ungrateful bastard, Doc Baggs, Judge Van Horne, and several more. Jeff accepted it, even if he didn't like it. The regulars and a couple of hard men like Yeah Mow would stick probably, but people like Yank and Syd were not fighters, either. There was no way around it. It was a bad hand, but he would have to play it anyway.

Chapter Twenty

Mattie heard the rumors, too. Whores were the real telegraph of the world and her girls were churning and anxious all day until some of the few customers they had complained. Mattie was in a mood herself and told them to go hop a toad.

As the sun passed over the mountain, the streets were quiet but not quite deserted. Occasionally people would huddle and look up, as if they expected to see something. The Tivoli was kept going although the clientele was slim and some of the boys had to play against each other. Since they were all accomplished cheaters, this led to a certain rancor.

Mattie didn't come down for dinner with her girls, as was her custom. She remained in her room with a gruesome headache and a bottle of laudanum on the bedside table. Gradually the noise below faded and she was able to sleep.

About midnight there was a powerful pounding on her door. She thought at first that it was in her head, but an authoritative voice barked an order to open up.

She went prepared to curse whoever it was and was surprised to find Holy Moses, Cy Warman, and Cameron, all looking grave.

"Get a coat on Mattie and hurry it up."

"Why? What do you want?" Looking, she realized Moses was not his usual sartorial self for a town visit. All three were wearing rough clothes and were armed. "What's going on?"

"We're trying to protect you. Get some clothes on, dammit." Then Moses spoke to a clerkish young man wearing spectacles, standing behind him, directing him to get some of her things out of the closet and make it fast.

"You got your nerve, Mister Holier-Than-Thou Moses," Mattie said. "This is my house, god-dammit. You get out!"

The young man pushed past her, and, when Moses grabbed her wrists, there wasn't anything she could do but yell at him: "Hey, you wall-eyed bastard!" Moses pulled her to him, jammed a hand over her mouth, and started dragging her out and down the stairs. Gunfire sounded in the distance. He spoke rapidly and softly into her ear. "We're doin' it for Jeff. Least we can do."

They moved her outside where there was a light mist on the ground. She was handed over to a small, nervous-looking band of armed citizens. The minute they uncovered her mouth, she started to yell: "What have you done, Holy? Where's Jeff?"

"I don't know. Dead maybe."

She let out a shriek: "You bastard. You did this!"

With a hard, unforgiving look, he reminded her: "So did you, Miss Silks. At least what I did is for people besides myself."

That devastated Mattie. She was reduced to some muted sobs. The men were taking no chances and so gagged her with a bandanna.

Moses said he was going back into the house to try to get the girls out. As he went, Mattie heard him tell one of the men: "Things're gettin' out of hand. Gettin' mean."

The reddish hue on the horizon at the other end of town, along with gunshots and a lot of loud yelling, seemed to confirm it.

The man Moses had addressed complained to him: "We're not fighters, Holy, most of us."

"Don't I know it."

The men—she recognized most of them, but none wanted to acknowledge her at the moment—took her up into a small cañon off a back street where she had nothing to do but ponder how it was that these solid citizens thought they were doing Jeff a kindness by taking care of her? She knew it was crazy to think about it when obviously something catastrophic was going on, but she couldn't help herself. They, at least, thought Jeff loved her, or that was the implication. Had he said so to one of them or were they merely being intuitive? Either way, all this was so marvelous that she had completely forgotten a small detail, the object of this romantic epiphany might well be dead, and, if that was so, she might as well follow him there.

Some time back Jeff had moved to another hotel in the south end of town and kept his room even when, for a while, he had been spending most nights at Mattie's. He had been changing his clothes in preparation for the nightly tour of his establishments when he heard the first indications of war. It wasn't an unfamiliar sound, a bunch of rambunctious cowboys wahooing a main street—in their parlance putting the "town up a tree". Except this wasn't a cattle town. His well-known, absolutely honed instincts told him it was far more dire.

He strapped on the Colt but, in his haste, forgot the rifle before going out, hurrying downstairs and out into the street. He wasn't there long; it was too dangerous. Men were breaking into shops and storehouses, living quarters and saloons, but not, he noted looking up the street, into the Exchange, although its front entrance was once again open. He saw two dead bodies and some buildings and tents on fire. Creede had a perilous history with fire, and, if they weren't controlled, it was likely the whole town would go up eventually. As of now, no one was interested in trying. Keeping his black suit in fog and shadow as much as possible, Jeff reconnoitered a short way to the north—the violence seemed to be coming from that direction.

He recognized a couple of Ford's cowboys—Pony Bill and Cale—but others were strangers to him. There didn't seem a focus to their destruction so far, just a bunch of Saturday night drunks enjoying riding around shooting off their pistols and raising general hell. But it didn't take him long to understand it was far worse than that and would soon engulf everyone and everything in Creede.

Ford was back and this was the only thing he had ever been good at. The way he would think was to destroy the town in order to own it. Smith had to wonder what had given him the courage? He thought of Mattie and turned on his heel to head back south at a trot, weaving in and out of the emptied buildings and tents. When he got to the Tivoli, a few of his boys were standing out in the street trying to see, looking north, speculating—Fatty with a bottle in his hand, dead-faced Yeah Mow holding his hatchet, Yank jumping around and gesticulating. They rightfully looked worried but nobody was doing anything.

Jeff stopped long enough to rail at them: "Arm yuhrselves yuh damn' fools, and get down to the Library! It'll be easier to defend. Get there an' put up some barricades an' douse the lamps. It's Ford . . . they're comin' tuh kill yuh, for Christ's sake!"

Everyone scuttled. Jeff ran on to the Library where the girls were either fleeing or wandering around like a disturbed herd, hugging each other, unsure whether they should be thrilled by the spectacle or terrified by its promise. A couple ran to greet Jeff, begging for some direction. He told them to get out and pointed the way—coincidentally the same direction

Holy's bunch had taken Mattie.

Smith found Syd in the dark at the far end of the porch, sharing an opium pipe with a Chinese whore named Golden Eyes, both oblivious, too far into the dream to care. Storming at him, he grabbed the pipe out of Syd's mouth, threw it off the porch, and slapped Syd in the face several times. When the whore objected, he slapped her, too. There was no sign that either felt it. In fact, Syd grinned and said: "My ol' pard, Soapy . . . hi ya. . . ."

Syd was grabbed, picked up, and thrown bodily after the pipe to land forcefully on the hard ground, and that purchased at least a modicum of the gentleman's attention. Jeff then relented, went down off the porch to lift him up, and held him there. The gang was streaming into the Library now, passing the remaining whores who were making a run for it, the sober supporting the drunk and drugged.

As the last of the girls ran out, Jeff intercepted one at the foot of the steps. "Where's Mattie?"

Two huge, water-filled deer eyes stared at him. "What's happening, Jeff? Everybody's scared to death. I don't know where to go."

He told her—"That way."—but maintained his fierce grip. "Where's Mattie?"

"I don't know, honest. Somebody said Holy came with some men and took her."

"He knew," Jeff said aloud to himself, biting it off, but then: "Why Mattie?" He knew the only thing Holy loved was silver.

He had forgotten that he was holding the girl in a painful grip. "Can I go now, please?" she pleaded. "That's all I know. Holy came in and told us all to get out, but most of the girls didn't understand."

Jeff freed her and she ran off after the others, clunking

along awkwardly in her high-heeled boots. He figured that she would probably find most of respectable Creede and her sisters hiding in the cañon by now.

Up on the porch, Golden Eyes had retrieved the pipe and was looking down at him with an addict's superior smile. She sang languidly but in a surprisingly little girl's voice:

> The cliffs are solid silver,
> With wondrous wealth untold,
> And beds of the running rivers
> Are lined with the purest gold. . . .

Inside the Library, the lights had been extinguished and there was a lot of banging and smashing of furniture as barricades were being built. Jeff went in to remind them to bring in buckets of water from the pump in back. Not being of the sort who owned ammunition belts, none of them had brought a sufficient supply, and among the superfluity of useless weapons was a collection of knives, saps, and brass knuckles. Syd, still dreaming, at least had his Derringer out, prepared no doubt to fight to the death with it. There were only two rifles among them, but Fatty had his shotgun.

As the tide of destruction grew closer, Jeff went out onto the porch to watch, kneeling behind the balustrade. Golden Eyes at the other end was still puffing away and singing in her sad little voice:

> While the world is filled with sorrow,
> And hearts must break and bleed,
> It's day all day in the daytime,
> And there is no night in Creede.

It was so macabre Jeff didn't know whether to laugh or get

mad. Still, he wouldn't do anything to stop her; everyone dealt with their nightmares in their own way. As it turned out, it wasn't up to him anyway.

He heard the *crack* of the shot but had no idea where it had come from. There weren't any horsemen out front as yet. Golden Eyes had been about to begin another chorus, her pretty mouth opening to form the first syllable—"It"—when, instead, she gasped, sighed, and slipped down quietly in the big, high-backed rattan chair. It looked as though someone had flung a Chinese doll there.

Jeff looked up as several men headed his way on foot and horseback, firing generally at the Library as they moved down the street. His own men replied with a furious barrage from the windows on both floors, while he dodged inside, swearing fervently at them about saving their meager supply of bullets. That was a difficult concept for men accustomed to saloon and street fights where everything was decided in minutes if not seconds.

Syd, coming out of the drug a little, grabbed Jeff's sleeve. "Where's Golden Eyes?"

"Dead. Damn' fool sat out there singin' that blessed song, an' they shot her."

His explanation had been delivered staccato. He had bigger concerns and failed to note the effect the news had on Syd.

Syd's mind drifted for a moment, but then, by sheer will, he forced himself back into the present. Still somewhat hazy, he lurched to the front door. Without even looking, he plunged out onto the porch with nothing but his two-shot Derringer in his hand. He saw Golden Eyes crumpled there, at the end of the porch where he had left her, the pipe still smoking at her feet. Taking fumbling steps in her direction, he started for her. Kelly came riding furiously around the opposite end of the house, right up to the porch before Syd could react.

Everything in slow motion, Syd tried feebly to raise the Derringer, cursing Kelly for the girl's death, no matter who had shot her. From a few feet away, Kelly pointed his long-barreled Navy Colt and fired from the saddle, two rapid rounds straight into his chest. Syd said—"Aw, damn. . . ."— and died right there.

Kelly dug in the spurs and rode off crazily, shouting incoherently to celebrate his victory. Some people said later, it gave them the chills. Jeff came running out in time to fire a shot at Kelly's disappearing back, but missed. He jammed his gun in the holster and dragged Syd back inside.

They laid him on a divan in the parlor. Jeff looked around. The besieged were a sorry lot. Jeff had not realized until this moment that Yeah Mow still intended to fight the enemy with his hatchet, disdaining firearms. He had to be ordered to take one of the two rifles. Fatty had his shotgun and a .38 and was competent with either one, but then the list grew thin.

Bowers was upstairs, figuring to loot the place. Finding him, Jeff grabbed him roughly and told him, if he wanted to be useful, to go downstairs and say a prayer over Syd—if he knew any. Banjo now had the other rifle and was guarding the back. One of the dealers from the Tivoli, not even a member of the gang, and the kid who had brought Jeff the lynching message, had come along out of simple loyalty, making Jeff feel a little better about dying in such company.

The raiders began to surround the building and move in closer, firing so many rounds into it that Jeff's men could do little else than hug the furniture or the floor. There was no shortage of ammunition out there. Between gusts of gunfire, cries were heard, Kelly's voice prominent among them. "Come out an' fight, yellow bellies! We want Soapy! Send out

Smith!" They even called him "Reb" when they couldn't think of anything else. Mostly they were gathering in front where they had pushed a couple of wagons close to the house and manned them with enough guns to repress any outcoming fire. When they got bored with shooting the Library into kindling, they would storm the place and there would be very little to stop them.

Cale got overly excited and rode boldly up to the porch in imitation of Kelly, firing into the windows. Fatty used his shotgun to blow the cowboy five feet out of the saddle. The horse ran back the way it had come.

They could hear Ford's men cursing the death of one of their own, but no one attempted to retrieve the body—they merely increased their rate of fire. Fatty took a scalp wound and another in the bulk of his hip but hardly seemed to notice. In back, Banjo was hit in the arm and, after bandaging it, found it a little stiff and painful but still usable. He stayed at his post without mentioning it to anyone.

Ford wasn't to be seen, but inside the Library they heard his voice—"Burn it!"—and got the message. It turned out that the Smith's gang had only been able to find five buckets in which to keep water against this eventuality. It didn't take long before they could see lanterns being lit at various points. Several were thrown but fell short and burned out.

The first besieger to try and get closer thought he would be safer around the side, but the dealer, using a Browning, shot him in the groin just as he was about to throw the lantern. Screaming and clutching himself, the incendiary fell to the ground and rolled. The lantern spilled out its guts harmlessly on the dirt and slowly burned out while the man tried to crawl away, leaving a bloody stain on what would have been a lawn if there had been one in Creede.

The next to try it, from in front, threw farther and more

accurately. The lantern landed on the wooden porch where it flared and blossomed. Jeff was checking how many bullets they had left and not finding the prospect rosy when he heard the lantern explode.

"Soapy," Yank asked plaintively, staring at the spreading fire on the porch as if hypnotized, "you think we're gonna get out of this one? I wanted to leave my poems to my mother, but I kept puttin' it off. . . ."

"Damned if I know," was all Jeff could tell him, but he grinned in spite of everything. At the moment, he didn't have a way out of the situation, not that he had ever stopped trying to come up with one. He thought he saw a shape behind the flames, got off a hasty shot through one of the broken front windows, and was rewarded with what sounded like a yelp of pain and cursing.

The fire had spread across the front, shattering what was left of the windows, cutting off visibility, and driving the gang to the inside wall of the parlor and beyond. Jeff dragged Syd's body with him as they retreated. Bullets and a seemingly endless stream of primitive cries and invective came from the other side of the inferno, but the men inside had no way of returning fire. Some of the voices rising over the crackling flames were eerie in their barbarous celebration, promising several kinds of terrible death to their enemies. They howled names—"Soapy", of course, the main target, "Fat Man", "Bag-a-Bones" (Yank), "Chinaman", "Big Mouth" (Bowers)—and taunted them, dared them to come out.

"Soapy, you think that Holy Moses and them'll maybe come to help?" Fatty asked, with his usual total lack of emotion.

"I'm not countin' on it," Jeff answered.

"What are we countin' on?" Bowers asked, holding a pistol now but as if it were a pocket comb, his pockets bulging with cash and jewels. When he saw Jeff giving the cache a dubious look, he said: "I can't have people sayin' I died broke."

"Lookin' forward to that, are you?" Jeff said. He had misplaced his sense of humor. "Farther back in the house," he ordered. "Back!"

They moved through the dining room and the sun parlor—called the "sin parlor" locally—and finally to the large kitchen and pantry. Smoke was pouring through the house, making it hard to breath and even harder to talk.

"We're gonna have tuh go for it, boys," Jeff managed to squeeze out, choking. "Out the back here."

"We'll get kilt, for sure," the usually phlegmatic Banjo Parker said. "That's where they shot me from . . . look." He indicated his wound.

"I know, but if we run like hell, shoot at ever'thin' in sight, some of us might make it tuh the rocks. God knows, Banjo, maybe somebody'll take pity, but that's all I got to offer." Jeff stood up in the ever denser smoke, coughing, tears running, struggling to get out his words. "There's somethin' I been meanin' to say, an' I'll tell yuh right now"—he grinned and reached out to grab their hands one by one as they crowded around—"I wouldn't've missed a day of it."

Chapter Twenty-One

The shooting in front of the house suddenly took on a crescendo—furious bursts of rifle fire interspersed with confused yelling and screams of pain.

"I been hit, I been hit, god dammit!"

"Help me, help me!"

"Die game, brother."

"They got my horse!"

The words were hard to distinguish clearly from the back of the building, cut off as Smith's gang was, pressing away from the heat. The cause for all that confusion out front was even more difficult to understand. Yet something strange was happening, something none of them could grasp. If the battle had been music, this was a whole new tune in another key, and one that went on and on.

One family of shots sounded steady, almost rhythmic: Remington and Winchester rifles. The other firing—there was more of it, if you knew how to listen—was largely from pistols, but wilder and more disconnected.

"Herky-jerky!" Bowers said.

"I don't know what the hell's goin' on out there," Jeff decided, "but it's better'n fryin' in here."

Led by Jeff, the men charged out the back door, fully expecting to be shot down or at least shot at. Nothing happened. The area was empty of hostiles, deserted.

They stood there for a moment, stunned just at being alive, but then a rallied Jeff directed them around the side of the burning building in time to see Ford's raiders fleeing up the main street on foot and horseback. It was a rout, but why? There were six bodies scattered around the front of the burning Library, two more wounded—one gut-shot and sitting up, and the other trying to crawl away. Jeff knew Fatty had got one and he thought he might have gotten another. Outlaws did not fight to the death for anyone, and then only if cornered. Ten men down would be more casualties than any gang could endure.

The answer to Jeff's question materialized out of the fog and foliage across the street: six battered but triumphant warriors shuffling forward, grinning. Ed Dooley had been hit in both arms and was a little wobbly, needing help to stand tall, but still clinging to his rifle with one hand, even as blood ran down that arm and along the barrel.

Jeff went to meet Dooley, while the rest of his gang just stood there, bewildered, dazed by it all.

"I'll be god damned," Jeff said, "if I ever been happier tuh see enna one in mah whole life than yuh boys." He looked around in amazement at the destruction they had brought to the raiders. "How in hell . . . ?"

One of the Southerners, the youngest, brandished his Winchester proudly by way of explanation.

"Like huntin' anything," Dooley said, "lie in wait, real patient, and, when yuhr time comes, shoot good . . . you cain't go wrong. Donnie here can hit the eye of uh rabbit or squirrel at a fer piece. I seen him do it many a time."

It was apparent that Dooley was exhausted and running out of steam. Jeff shouted for Yank to come over and do what he could for the man's wounds and for someone to find some blankets and maybe that jackass of a doctor, if he was still alive. They helped Dooley to lie down on the ground, but he wouldn't give up the rifle.

Jeff took off his own jacket and propped it under the man's head. Kneeling next to him and close, he spoke softly: "I thought yuh boys went back home."

"Wal, tuh be truthful with yuh, Mister Smith, seein' the line uh business yuh're in, we didn't know if we could 'xactly trust yuh. I'm sorry 'bout that."

Jeff told him not to worry. He had to force himself not to smile at the irony that cohorts of Jesse James and the Youngers didn't trust him because of *his* "line uh business".

Dooley's voice was down to a whisper and full of regret. "Didn't git ol' Ford, though, an' that's what we come for."

Jeff said he'd "be got", and it was his to see to. Kneeling there, he checked to see that he had a full chamber.

Dooley tugged at his sleeve and pushed his rifle toward him. "Take it, Mister Smith. Only single shot but it shoots true. I seen the Remington that Kelly had pull to the right." He fumbled some shells out of a pocket and pushed them along the ground with his bloody fingers.

Jeff looked at the rifle and wasn't even sure of the make, it looked old but in fine condition. He touched the blood on the barrel with his finger, an anointment.

"For Cousin Jesse," the Southerner said, his voice cracking.

"For Cousin Jesse."

Without saying anything to anyone, Jeff stood and strode off, heading up the ravaged, burning street where dust from the Ford gang's flight still mingled with the smoke. He passed another outlaw body on the way and thought it looked like Pony Bill. A dog was sniffing at the corpse, and Jeff, leery of its intentions, chased it away.

Ahead lay Ford's Exchange, one of the few undamaged buildings, dark and seemingly deserted with the windows still boarded up, looming over the ruined town like an exhausted beast over its prey, trying to decide what to do with it. In Ford's second story office window, the shade was drawn. It moved slightly, but Jeff was still at such a distance that it went undetected.

A horse wandered on the loose a couple of blocks ahead. A man came out of the burning livery stable, threw a bucket of water on the flames but, when he caught sight of Jeff striding up the street toward him with the rifle cradled under his arm, ducked back inside.

Suddenly there was life in the entrance to the Exchange. Kelly stepped out into the street, only a silhouette with the fires behind him but distinctive in his swagger. Jeff would have known him anywhere; there was that between them. He was carrying his rifle high.

Jeff had to calculate the distance between them carefully. Not being a famous shot himself, he wanted to get as close as possible. On the other hand, Kelly was a good shooter and let everyone know it. He was the first to fire, raising the rifle to his shoulder and pulling the trigger without a lot of aiming— typical arrogance. It churned up the dirt near Jeff's feet— nothing to be proud of.

Jeff knelt, aimed carefully, fired . . . and missed.

Kelly looked aside as if it had come close—men did that even when they couldn't possibly have heard or seen sign of the bullet. Jeff stood quickly and went forward again, a step at a time, by sheer force of will. Any hurry, any anxiety on his part would be a betrayal of himself.

Kelly, remaining in place, took a little longer in aiming this time and the bullet went through Jeff's shirt sleeve, putting a burn on his upper arm but without severe damage. He flexed it once to see how it was working but disdained looking at it. Kneeling quickly, he started to reload when he heard one, two, three shots aimed at him, buzzing around his ears, and looked up to find Kelly marching defiantly toward him on a slant, firing on the move. It was difficult to walk and aim at the same time, but Kelly had plenty of shells in that magazine and could afford to count on saturating the target.

Jeff, moving hastily, fumbled a little getting the shell into the chamber and almost jammed it. He cursed himself and took a deep breath before putting the loaded rifle to his shoulder, this despite two more rounds coming from the Remington, one of which hit his thigh. He felt the shock but barely winced, so intent was he. A faucet drip of blood appeared, one after the other, darkly on black pants.

In those few seconds he had to accept that he was presenting himself as an easy target, gritting his teeth against the prospect of being struck mortally, trying to remember how Earp had always said that in gunfights it was nerve that won out. Who shot first wasn't anywhere as important as who shot well. Now, for some reason, it was Kelly who froze in the middle of the street, halting his advance, leaning forward, and staring as if in wonder that his enemy was still fighting, but at the same time stuffing more shells into his rifle

Jeff took careful aim, pulled the trigger back slowly, smoothly, fired, and blew Kelly off his feet. He spun in the dirt a couple of times, howling, but then lurched back up to stand defiantly straight, blood all over his denim shirt so that it was impossible to know where he had been hit. He dropped the rifle, pulled his pistol, and began to stagger forward until it became a run, a lion charging straight at his enemy, firing wildly.

It was another equally desperate test of nerve, but Jeff had passed the crisis point. He loaded quickly and efficiently, fired, and again dropped Kelly, whose last sound was more of a squeal than a howl. He fell back and lay there. His boots twitched a couple of times, but, after that, he was quiet as ashes. A dog began howling; they always seemed to know.

It began to rain again, but gently, more of a drizzle that complemented the fog. Jeff, cautious, trying to think clearly, remained where he was for a moment, examining his wounded thigh. There was a lot of blood, but he didn't want to take the time to bandage it. A lucky thing, that pause, for someone else fired at him from a high angle, and, had the shooter been closer, there was no doubt in his mind he would have been hit. As it was, the bullet opened his boot but without striking the flesh.

He ducked involuntarily and then ran, limping and dodging, for the cover of a burning store. The shot had come from the direction of the Exchange. Jeff looked up at the black rectangle of the second-story window, stared at it long, knowing the man behind the shade would have to move it sometime, and he did—a tiny movement, seeking his hunter.

Before Jeff could load and raise the rifle, any sign of a presence behind the window disappeared. He propped Dooley's rifle against a wall, pulled his pistol, and, embracing walls, fiery and otherwise, ran for the entrance to the Exchange. There, sheltered from above by the porch roof, he took a deep breath, checked the chambers of his pistol again although he had yet to fire it, and considered a charge through the front door, figuring Ford wouldn't be on the first floor, anyway, and it would be dark inside.

He reconsidered, then loped and gimped around to the back entrance, instead. Kicking the door open, he rushed inside to find himself under the balcony that led to Ford's upstairs office. Jeff stopped and pressed himself back against the wall beneath it where he was somewhat sheltered by stacks of tables and gambling equipment that had been pushed aside.

There was a noise directly above him, not much of one, a tiny *clanging,* but he gambled, firing three fast, well-spaced shots through the floor of the balcony. Not a sound came back, but dust settled on and around him. He could see faint light through the holes but no sign of life.

The casino floor was desolate, unkempt, some chairs lying on their sides as if thrown there, a table on its back with the four legs sticking up like some dead animal in *rigor mortis*, the only real light coming from the door he had just kicked in and some of the cracks and crevices typical of construction in Creede. The bar was absent of bottles but there were a couple of dirty glasses sitting there with cobwebs on them. Jeff settled onto his haunches, ignoring the pain, and tried to think it through.

His leg was starting to get a little numb below the place where it had been hit, although he could feel the blood as it crept down his leg. The other wound, to his arm, seemed to hurt out of all proportion to the damage. Maybe some of it was the fact that he was terribly fatigued and suffering from nerves. He wished he knew that Mattie was all right.

He wondered if Ford had thrown something from his office out onto the balcony in order to lure him into doing just what he had done, reveal his position. If so, he was still upstairs, his office being the only room on the second floor. On the other hand, it could have been thrown from almost anywhere, something light such as a coin. It only had to land above Jeff to make itself heard. Should he try the stairs, creep up or make a grand charge, go right after him in his lair? That was his impulse. And because it was, he decided against it. Impulses were for men like Ford.

Thinking that his prey might just as easily be down on the first floor quite close to him, Jeff decided to try the same game—that would be unexpected. His first thought was to pitch his damaged boot, but he decided that it was too heavy and cumbersome and might be taken for exactly what it was, a thrown boot. He had left his coat under Dooley's head. Albeit dirtied and smudged by ash, his shirt still showed white and might be a little too easy to see with him in it. He stripped it off and wadded it around his large gold watch for weight.

Then he had an inspiration. He remembered that on his only trip up and down those stairs, they had creaked like a rheumatic old man. Already under the staircase, he got down on his hands and knees and crawled along the floor to the beginning of its understructure, his chin pressed so low at the end it was practically in the dust. From beneath the stairs, he began to push each ascending step in turn, pausing to suggest caution, then on to the next, and was rewarded with a beautiful groaning sound from each. Moving backwards as his hands progressed above his head, he could only reach so far before he had to stop, his arms not being long enough. If Bob were anywhere close by, he hadn't taken the bait so far. Ford was canny at times like this; he would have had to be to have survived so long with so many enemies. It wouldn't do to underestimate him.

Holding his pistol with his damaged arm, Jeff hastened out away from the wall and threw the shirt and watch up where it landed on the thirteenth step. He could see the flash of white and heard the *thump* on the stairs even as he shifted his pistol rapidly to his good hand, ducked low to the floor, and spun to face the room.

Thirteen turned out to be Bob Ford's unlucky number. He sprang up from behind the bar and began firing at the stairs with his rifle—at what the world will never know. Jeff was not far away and he started firing carefully but relentlessly with his Colt, four rounds.

Ford turned and looked at his assailant, slightly open-mouthed. The expression on his face was so child-like in its surprise and confusion in finding Smith there that even to Jeff it seemed almost pathetic. Bob grunted, the only sound he made as two of Jeff's rounds struck home, one in the chest and the other in the neck. Hands gripping the edge fiercely, Ford sank beneath the level of the bar and disappeared, one tenacious hand the last thing to disappear.

Jeff wasn't going to expose himself until he had a good idea that his enemy was dead. He could hear breathing that didn't sound at all healthy. Outside was the crackling of some fires, distant shouts, a dog barking furiously, as if angered by all that had gone on. Inside, the eerie quiet seemed to go on forever. Bob's respiration was not the only sound violating it, Jeff realized, as he caught himself breathing in perfect synchronization with Ford. Jeff wondered if he were dying, too, although he couldn't think why.

Bob's abraded voice out of the darkness jolted him, echoes from the tomb, like something out of those seashells they sold at carnivals. Rasping, words coming slowly and with obvious effort, he said almost sadly: "You ought've stayed away from Creede, Smith. Ain't much of a place to die."

Jeff realized that it was meant not as his epitaph but rather was that of the man who had killed Jesse James and seen his name spread all over the world as a synonym for infamy. Sagging, so tired it was an effort to breath, Smith allowed himself to plop back down on the littered floor and sit.

With nothing else to do and faint of mind, he thought as to how maybe Bob was one of those creatures who would rather be spat upon by generations than leave no sign upon the earth that he had ever been here at all. There was something in that which Soapy Smith could understand.

Jeff was still sitting there, dazed and blunted by his wounds and just plain sensory overload, when Yank, Fatty, and Bowers found him. They were cautious about entering, but he heard them and called out. Each had to go over and look behind the bar to confirm for themselves that the famous Bob Ford was really dead, but, at first, none would touch him.

Yank retrieved Jeff's shirt from the stairs and put it on him as he was shivering, then tied off the arm and leg although the bleeding had pretty much stopped. Bowers gave him his coat, humming under his breath about the "dirty little coward who shot down Mr. Howard", now that its performance didn't carry the death penalty. Fatty had a bottle of whiskey, some of which was poured on the makeshift bandages and some down Jeff's throat. He began to revive, but the boys, nevertheless, insisted on carrying him back to the Library.

As they went through the devastated streets, the inhabitants were coming out and assessing the damage. Some were still putting out fires while others were already at work getting things back in order, even hammering and sawing. The durable citizenry of Creede had weathered worse fires and floods and were not easily discouraged. The whole town was so flimsy that there was little that couldn't be put back as it had been in very short time.

As the little convoy went back down the main street, they could see that roulette wheels and dice cages were prominent among the first things saved. If Jeff hadn't been so debilitated, he might have made a philosophical comment on that. As they passed, people would stop and stare. If they looked too interested, Fatty would give them his best glare and that discouraged comment.

One man, no doubt emboldened by his anxiety, asked somewhat timidly, certain he would receive a dire answer: "Where's Ford?"

Yank answered him in the language of the town—"Drew to a bob-tailed flush, ol' Bob did."—and left the man stunned and speechless. But as they went on, they could hear him at some distance shouting out the news to others. They could also hear in the responses how the news was greeted with excitement but considerable doubt. Wisely the meek weren't taking chances. No one would until they saw Ford in a pine box, propped against the half-constructed council building the next day.

The Library had not fared as badly as Jeff had expected. The rain had helped, of course, but a large number of citizens had come to fight that particular fire which was, after all, in the town's premier whorehouse. It was also the first building that the good people, who had fled into the nearby cañon, confronted when the firing had died down and they saw fit to return.

Someone had rescued a pool table and put it down right in front of the building. The doctor, made relatively sober by the drastic events of the evening, had been brought there and was treating patients on it. The green felt was now dark red. Jeff demanded to be set down as they approached the scene; he sure wasn't going to be carried in.

Under the trees from where they had launched their attack, the Southerners were preparing to ride out. Dooley was propped up, tied to the saddle, with one of the others leading his horse. No one could understand why they would ride off in the chilly near dawn after all they had been through, but Jeff could. They were tough as catgut and had had enough notoriety in their lives and didn't want it any more now than he did.

Dooley gave Jeff a pleading look as he rode down the street between a couple of the boys. Jeff put up his arms, ignoring the pain, and clenched Dooley's hands together like a victorious prize fighter and shook them. Dooley grinned back— Jeff realized that it was for the first time—and was led off, heading for that blessed place, "back home".

Yeah Mow, it turned out, had been hit where the neck meets the shoulder and was lying on a blanket, while Banjo sat on the ground next to him after having been treated. Both were smoking and, despite all the blood on Yeah Mow's shirt and the odd angle at which his head rested, he looked relatively hale.

Jeff started over to see them, but Mattie stepped out to intercept him. She was a little breathless, shaken but mostly sad, only too aware that what she had done was irredeemable. She had lost him. Still. . . .

The mobile members of the gang pulled back when they saw the two were going to meet. Jeff stopped in his tracks and watched her come to him, calling his name softly.

"Mattie," he said softly.

They came together and then simply stood there awkwardly, only too aware that people were watching. To break the awkwardness, they turned to look at the Library where bucket brigades were still working to reduce the damage, the girls pitching in, too.

When she turned back to Jeff, there were tears in her eyes. "It's my fault, all of it. I told Holy about the telegraph. I wanted back at you for how I hurt. I didn't know what he was going to do with it. Couldn't have imagined this." She made a butterfly sweep of her hand toward the devastated town. Reaching out tentatively to touch his shoulder, she begged for understanding. "I swear to God I didn't, Jeff."

He thought for a minute, looking down at his wounded boot, then up to say: "I don't s'pose Holy did, neither. I guess ol' Bob just had too much in his craw tuh do ennathin' else. I put him up that tree mahself, an' I never knew. So I 'spect I carry a good amount uh fault there. Anyhow, he's 'crost the plain now."

"Ah," she said.

"We-all'd best just forget it."

"You can't forgive me, I know."

"I don't guess the boys'd let me."

"They do come first," she said, facing reality.

"Folks say I never threw a friend, an' I want 'em tuh be able tuh keep on sayin' it. Be mah epitaph."

"I understand that now." She looked him right in his black eyes with a skewed little smile. "I love you, Jeff."

He shook his head and topped her smile. "I love yuh, too, Mattie. But it don't mean a thing, does it?"

"No . . . no." Choked up, she broke off and hurried away to inspect the damage to her establishment.

No sooner than Mattie was out of the way, Yank and Fatty gathered up Jeff and placed him on the pool table for the doctor's inspection. The arm wound needed only cleaning, but the thigh still held fragments of Kelly's shot that had to be removed. There was no anesthetic, the ether having been used up, so Jeff drank an unaccustomed amount of whiskey. The procedure began under somewhat unusual conditions as Fatty kept the muzzle of a Colt .45 in the sawbones' ear, guaranteeing a successful result. The poor man, already suffering sobriety, winced but bore up because he didn't have any choice, at least until Jeff noticed the gun and told Fatty to put it away.

Holy Moses came over to talk to Jeff while he was lying there. "I'm sorry about your partner. I mean it. I liked Syd."

"Who would've thought," Jeff said between grunts and groans and without looking at Moses, "a little joke like that telegraph could come to burn a whole town and kill a whole lot uh folks. People generally take it better."

"Maybe we should have," Moses said heavily, and left.

"Day late an' a dollar short," Jeff murmured to the doctor.

210

* * * * *

As the strange dawn came on, beating its way up the mountains that hemmed in the ruined town, reddened by smoldering fires and tinted by the smoke, the Soapy Smith gang gathered to wait behind the Library where Syd's body had remained, although now propped up by the girls on some rescued chairs. To anyone else but this bunch it would have appeared grotesque.

Golden Eyes's corpse had been burned in the conflagration that followed her death, so the doctor had wrapped her remains tightly in a blanket, tied it off, and placed it well away from everyone until a coffin was made. Banjo and Fatty had told the local carpenter, whose job it was, that no matter what jobs were offered him, coffins were the priority.

At the cemetery on Boot Hill, Jeff, consistent with the gang's code, leaned over the box bearing the body of his friend and extracted several items from the always elegant suit. He gave the pearl-handled Derringer to Fatty where it disappeared in a meaty hand, the gold watch to Bowers, the diamond stickpin to Yank. He divided Syd's considerable roll between the two more severely wounded, Banjo and Yeah Mow.

During the service itself, the gravediggers had to work madly just a few feet away in order to get more holes finished in time. Bowers, holding a tattered Bible he never tired of carrying and seldom got around to consulting, did manage to come up with a fractured prayer and a couple of quotes that might have been found in the Good Book and were possibly attributable to the Psalms. The sealed coffin of Golden Eyes lay beside Syd's, although it was unlikely they had ever shared more than a pipe.

Eventually Bowers got around to addressing the Almighty,

man-to-man. "Lord, we're sending you up the souls of Gentleman Syd and a young lady of our rough acquaintance who called herself Golden Eyes."

Jeff heard some crying behind him and turned around to determine its source. Mattie, standing near her buggy, had arrived with her girls to mourn, and they went at it with some enthusiasm. She was obviously trying to keep them between Jeff and herself and seemed so uncharacteristically timid that it made Jeff sad. As well as she knew him, she ought to have known him better.

"Git on with it, Rev," he told Bowers.

"It's likely nobody knew Golden Eyes's name. But you'll know her, Lord, like you know all her sisters in trade. Well, for one thing she was a China girl, but a real sweet one. And you'll know the burdens she had to bear." He turned to the open coffin. "Syd Dixon was a gentleman and our friend. Maybe that isn't much to recommend him. But down here it seemed like a lot. Syd came to know that the 'way of the transgressor is hard . . . to quit'. They're both Yours now, Lord, and maybe they can get to know each other better up there. Be merciful. Amen."

A chorus of Amens and an outbreak of serious sobbing followed. Yank told Bowers it was the most beautiful burial service he had ever attended and was almost worth dying for. Fatty hit Bowers on the back, knocking out The Rev's wind. The little party wound its way down the hill to town. Other funerals were waiting to get started.

Jeff and Mattie never did meet face-to-face on that occasion or any other.

Later, back in town, out of his own pocket, Smith would give the dealer and the kid who had stood with them a thousand dollars apiece. He knew the dealer was called Ed, but he never did get the kid's name. When the boy looked at the thousand in hundreds, he passed out, which brought a lot of guffaws on that otherwise bleak morning.

The Tivoli had no roof and only three walls, one of them being propped up even as it opened for business that evening. Business was good, too. A couple of the gang members, who had run away, hadn't gone far and were back. Jeff forgave them as he forgave everyone, and would have forgiven Bob Ford for being Bob Ford if the son-of-a-bitch had ever given him a chance.

All the hale gang members were hustling some game or mark, leaving Jeff to stand alone at the bar and regard with some pride what God and he had managed—survival. That is, until Moses joined him in standing there and looking around.

"I got to hand it to you, Jeff, not much gets you down."

"Not till now."

Moses nodded, looking unhappy. "I figured you'd know."

"What?"

Moses, no coward, met his eyes. "Time for you and the boys to go, Jeff. Past time, maybe."

Jeff hummed but there was no sign of temper. "Yuh don't think maybe yuh owe us somethin'?"

"We do. I been around to the other mine owners all day, seeing how they feel, and we're giving you close on seven thousand dollars."

Jeff laughed, but it wasn't an engaging laugh, not even re-assuring. "We make more'n that 'round here in a single day, Holy. Ennaways, I wasn't speakin' uh money."

"I knew you weren't. But that's all we've got to give. With a little more time, we might raise it some, but it don't change the fact that you've got to go."

"An' what makes you think so?"

213

"We've been asking people and they want another kind of town. This last night made a lot of 'em unhappy. You lost your support with the public here, is, I guess, the way you'd have to put it."

"We-all didn't wahoo this town last night, shoot an' burn it. That was a fella named Bob Ford, 'member him."

"Feeling is . . . wouldn't have happened if you weren't here."

"Yuh wanted us here tuh get rid of him."

"Oh, we'd've done that ourselves, sooner or later. We were just waiting for him to overstep himself so town opinion'd turn against him and he'd have no choice. That's called politics."

"It surely is."

"A party went out this afternoon to ask for some federal marshals. It's in the national interest to protect the silver, you see. Some talked with Masterson about being sheriff. That'd depend on you going, of course." He paused, giving it weight. "You know I'm right, don't you?"

Jeff sighed. "I've seen it enough."

The gang didn't argue. They had "seen it enough" themselves to know when it was their time. That kind of disappointment was innate, built into their lives and souls.

Jeff decided they would go on their own terms, at least, and, oh, a grand leave-taking it was. A real carnival some people called it, and not a few regretted afterward that they had sent this riotous bunch away. It took Jeff three days to get an orchestra together, the best duds for the boys, candy for the kids, and little presents for the girls, flags and banners.

Cameron stood on a jerry-rigged platform and made a brief speech. "We'll miss this bunch like we miss a steam calliope at the circus after it's gone. But things are getting settled here now, and we have to run Creede along new lines if it's going to be a city. We're calling a halt to the rough stuff, that's the thing."

He went on to read off the conditions of their exile and recite each name in turn: "The following confidence men, sharpers, and bunco artists are hereby proscribed and required to be out of Creede by sundown of this day, never to return under penalty of durance vile or the short end of a rope.

"Randolph Jefferson 'Soapy' Smith. . . ."

From atop his latest white horse, Jeff tipped his hat and saluted the crowd.

"The Reverend Charles O. Bowers . . . Henry Edwards called Yank Hank Fewclothes. . . ."

As they marched past and were announced, they took their bows and moved on, out of the history of Creede.

All this was carried out in good high spirits with a lot of laughter, the gang waving little American flags, their derbys or stovepipes, packs of cards, saps, anything as they marched past the reviewing stand. Jeff led the way out of town like the general of a victorious army. As a known patriot, he saluted every flag.

The only person who wasn't treating this as a celebration was Mattie, sitting alone in her buggy well behind the crowd. Jeff looked over the heads and saw her. He recovered his rôle quickly, though, straightening in the saddle. Not so Mattie, who had no rôle.

Gradually the sound trailed away, as does the memory of men. The last of the gang disappeared into the trees leaving behind a silent, respectable town.

A year later Wall Street and the "Goldbugs" of the East

had their way with Congress through the Sherman Silver Act. The once precious metal was demonetized and fell from a dollar twenty-nine an ounce to fifty cents. Creede was doomed. Just as Soapy Smith had predicted.

Epilogue

Oh, I know how you probably heard Bob Ford was killed by a mysterious stranger named O'Kelly from down South somewheres, and he was the avenger of Jesse and was almost lynched and went to prison and all that. Wasn't true. See, the journalists of our day were more interested in the excitement of a thing than the facts. Facts didn't draw a lot of interest back then. Not sure they do now.

I do believe some honestly confused Dooley with that trail dirt, Rincón Kelly, but mostly it was Cy Warman, well-thought-of editor and publisher of the *Creede Candle* who thought enough of Jeff to keep him out of the killing side of it. While everybody knew Jeff liked attention and reputation and aspired to a lot of things, being known as the man who killed the man who killed Jesse James was not one of them.

Now you probably want to know what happened after. We already told you how the silver lost its luster. These business people always think they're so clever, but it takes a good sharper to know the future. That's because their lives are so chancy, they got nothing to fall back on, so they just got to be smarter. Soapy Smith read more newspapers, and probably more books, than anyone in Creede.

Mattie married Holy Moses, or James Madison Moses as he styled himself later, and they moved to Denver where she regularly attended the opera in a fancy carriage and gave "evenings at home" that had every swell in town fighting to get in.

One night as she was going home through the streets, she heard a familiar voice with a familiar pitch. Her heart did somersaults, I tell you, and she ordered the carriage to stop and ran back. Holy—as we knew him—lit a cigar and sat back to wait. He had heard it, too.

"How you fixed for soap, boys, how are you fixed for soap . . . ?"

When she caught up with the voice, it was surrounded by a sparse and not very interested crowd, but her heart started running again when she saw it was Bowers. Still, it left her frozen there with high feelings. The Rev looked down and, when he saw her, broke off his pitch in mid-sentence, leaving the onlookers, the potential marks, restless and wondering what was up.

Yank Hank, working the crowd, spotted her and came over. She had tears in her eyes.

"Hello, Yank."

"Hello, Mattie. Good to see you. You look fine."

Bowers started up again in the background: "Win fifty, win a hundred, how can you lose? Take my word as a man of the cloth, brethren, cleanliness is next to godliness and almost as good as a sawbuck in the hand. . . ."

Mattie, getting a second look at Bowers, thought he appeared a little seedy, and Yank seemed as though he might have come to believe his own blarney about the virtues of honey—in other words, drawn through a knothole. But then she had gained a few pounds and had added a couple of lines to her face.

Yank was obviously waiting for the question she didn't dare ask. "Jeff . . . ," was all she got out.

"Jeff's dead. Killed last June up in Skagway."

"Ah."

"But, oh, Mattie, we had ourselves a time till it happened.

He finally got it all. They called him King of Skagway. Four days before they killed him, he was Grand Marshal of the Fourth of July parade, carrying a big flag on one of those big white horses he loved, and, oh, how they cheered him. It was grand."

It was too much for Mattie. She started to cry while Yank looked on helplessly, hands flapping at his sides. She turned and hurried away.

Bowers watched her go even as he continued with his pitch: "Now who'll take a chance? Step right up. Who'll take a chance?"

When Mattie got back into her carriage, she was still crying, but Moses never asked her why and knew better than to put his arm around her. He always was a gentleman.

Now with all the myth-making that goes on about the West and the things we did, you can believe that if you want to. There's another version and you can take it or leave it. See, they didn't call us confidence men for nothing. We had our ways. People up there in Skagway who cared about Soapy got a little worried about him—about his drinking which he never did much of before, and him starting to believe his own myth and feeling invulnerable, like kings are supposed to. They knew there was a vigilante committee, headed up by an engineer named Reid, that was out to get him. Reid especially had a hair up his behind when it came to Soapy. So, when Soapy announced to everyone that he would go alone to the vigilante meeting the next night and face them down, the boys knew they had to take steps.

It was nothing to get into Reid's rooms and replace the ammunition in the rifle he always carried with blank cartridges. A good thing, too, for what the gang had feared might happen the next night down on the town wharf did happen. There was a confusion, an argument, and they shot each other, although Soapy had tried to stop it, yelling out the Maker's name and that he "didn't want this".

When the blank went off so close to Soapy, it burned him and he naturally thought he had been hit and fell to the ground. You know, like shell-shocked in the war. Then Yank, hanging 'way back with the rest of the boys because they had been so ordered, ran up and threw himself on top of Jeff, doing his grieving act, whispering for him to stay down and play dead.

Old Soapy came to his senses after that and decided just to disappear. Just like Butch did—hell, I was out there in Utah, sitting on the porch with Cassidy, watching the sunset, drinking from a jug, and spinning yarns only a couple years ago. Well, maybe it was five, or so. Or ten. I'll tell more of that next time, if I live long enough. Anyway, that's another of those myths you can take or leave, suit yourself. And never mind who I am. Just get on with your damned pinhead lives. Suckers.

Author's Note

Yes, there certainly was a Randolph Jefferson "Soapy" Smith, and, save for a few politicians or generals who have stolen whole countries, he was without a doubt the greatest con man of modern times. The kind of "big stores" you saw in THE STING were very small beer compared to some of the bizarre capers Soapy's gang pulled off, and the latter lived in much rougher times where the play often had to be backed by guns and brass knuckles.

All of the elaborate cons utilized in this yarn have been reported somewhere, at least, to be absolutely true. There were others, equally amusing, but space and the dictates of story construction forced me to forego them.

The central characters except for Soapy's perennial deceivers, the city council, and Ford's vicious enablers are also real. Not that the "dirty little coward who shot down Mr. Howard" didn't have an ugly crew around him, but, to my knowledge, their names haven't come down to us. Naturally times and places have been maneuvered this way and that for the usual necessities drama brings to the table.

It's funny how, bright as he was, Jeff could never stop believing in his high-toned way that there was room in the coming civilization for his brand of rascally "entertainment". The "interests" invariably used the gang and their piquant view of law and order up to a point and then, when things prospered, ran them out. They say "you can't kid a kidder", although in my personal view the "boys" in their heart of hearts always knew this would be their fate and didn't care a lot—Gypsy blood came with the calling.

Much of the material for this book came from notes taken long, long ago, recorded with youthful enthusiasm but little attention given to details such as sources. The three books on my shelf at the moment are THE REIGN OF SOAPY SMITH by William Ross Collier and Edwin Victor Westrate, SOAPY SMITH, KING OF THE FRONTIER CON MEN by Frank Robertson and Beth Kay Harris, and HIGH JINKS ON THE KLONDIKE by Richard O'Connor.

Finally, I don't think I should speak to the whole question of who died when or where, or if they died at all. My sly, thoroughly cantankerous narrator has given us his view and I'm not going to argue with him. He already thinks I'm as big a pinhead as the rest of you.